D1529436

IN
MIKE
WE
TRUST

IN MIKE WE TRUST

P. E. RYAN

HARPER TEEN
An Imprint of HarperCollins*Publishers*

HarperTeen is an imprint of HarperCollins Publishers.

In Mike We Trust
Copyright © 2009 by P. E. Ryan
www.harperteen.com

Library of Congress Cataloging-in-Publication Data
Ryan, Patrick.
  In Mike we trust / P. E. Ryan. — 1st ed.
    p. cm.
  Summary: When Uncle Mike shows up for an extended visit, fifteen-year-old
Garth must decide if he can trust his somewhat secretive uncle, as he wrestles
with coming out, which he wants to do, but promised his mother he would wait.
  ISBN 978-0-06-085813-1 (trade bdg.)
  [1. Coming out (Sexual orientation)—Fiction. 2. Homosexuality—Fiction.
3. Mothers and sons—Fiction. 4. Uncles—Fiction. 5. Honesty—Fiction.
6. Swindlers and swindling—Fiction.] I. Title.
PZ7.R9555In 2009   2008011722
[Fic]—dc22   CIP
                                                                 AC

Typography by Alison Klapthor
09 10 11 12 13 CG/RRDB 10 9 8 7 6 5 4 3 2

First Edition

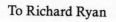

To Richard Ryan

Acknowledgments

Many thanks to Tara Weikum and Erica Sussman for their enthusiastic editorial guidance, and to Lisa Bankoff for being the best agent an author could ever hope to have.

And, as always, thank you to Fred Blair for his encouragement, his support, his presence.

1

They were just finishing dinner when they heard a screech of tires, followed by several taps of a car horn. The dog began to bark, and Garth's mom flinched and looked up from her plate. She glanced toward the window that opened onto the side street, then gave Garth the worried expression he'd grown so used to over the past year and a half. *Relax*, he wanted to tell her, *it's nothing*. They lived in the middle of Richmond, surrounded by other houses. Since when was the sound of a car horn a reason to flinch?

The furrow in her brow deepened at the sound of footsteps on the front porch, and she nearly dropped her fork when they heard the knock, same pattern as the horn.

"Who in the world could it be at this hour?" she asked, peering at the clock on the wall.

"I'll get it." Garth got up from the table and crossed through the living room, focusing on the tall, lanky shadow on the other side of the door's beveled glass. He shushed Hutch, who was circling his feet like a shark, and called out, "Who is it?"

"Santa Claus!" a voice said.

Garth looked back at his mom, then turned to the door again.

"Who?"

"Captain America! Come on, it's me! Open up!"

The voice sounded jovial and vaguely familiar. He undid the chain and the deadbolt, and eased the door open.

"Hey, hey, hey! Look at you, short stuff!"

At fifteen, Garth barely reached five feet two. He was aching for the growth spurt that seemed to have taken over all the other guys his age, and he *hated* being called "short stuff." He hated "shorty" and "shrimp" and "little bit," and he usually lashed out at anyone who used such nicknames. But he said nothing now. He stood frozen, amazed.

Standing before him—or so it seemed in that first, arresting moment—was his dad's ghost.

In general, Garth tried not to dwell on the accident. When he caught his mind drifting toward it, he would force himself, instead, to concentrate on his dad *before* the event, on the man Jerry Rudd had been. He made mental lists of attributes:

Well liked.

Calm spirited.

Hard worker.

Corny joke teller.

Sailing nut. That last one was how his dad had described himself, anyway. He'd loved sailing more than anything else and he'd dreamed of one day building his own boat "completely out of wood, like they did it in the old days—right down to the pegs that hold it together."

He'd never gotten the chance.

Garth didn't share his dad's passion for sailing, but he'd inherited—possibly by sheer will—his love of ships. In Garth's case, these were miniatures, usually made of plastic because the wooden models were so expensive. His room was filled with them. They were lined up along his windowsill and dominated his bookcase. The largest—a handsome, highly detailed *Batavia*—spanned the top of his dresser.

Most days, the ships made him feel connected to his dad, but the nights were a different matter entirely.

His recurring nightmare, he'd decided, was like being strapped into a movie seat in the front row of the scariest horror film imaginable. He was forced to watch, over and over again, his dad and his dad's friend, Mr. Holt, try to outrun the sudden storm on the Chesapeake Bay. The sailboat was a twelve-foot Sunfish. Mr. Holt was manning the tiller; Garth's dad was working the line for the sail. Always, in the nightmare, they were enjoying themselves at first. Even as the dark sky rained down on them, they joked about man versus nature. Then things turned serious—fast. They had to shout through the wind and the rain to hear each other. They tried one maneuver, then another, but nothing worked. There was a moment too awful for Garth to wrap his brain around wherein both men realized that, all jokes aside, they were up against a force they couldn't possibly beat.

And then it happened. In one version, the mast snapped off. In another (like last night's), the boat just turned sideways, sail and all, throwing his dad and Mr. Holt into the water. Either way, the ending was the same: they tried to cling to the sinking hull; they fought to survive. But eventually the stormy bay filled their lungs.

Just another nightmare, Garth always told himself as he tried to fall back to sleep. *Get it out of your head.* But there was no getting it out completely, because although he hadn't witnessed it, the accident was very real. His dad had been dead for over a year and a half. His body—along with Mr. Holt's—had been recovered in a search-and-rescue mission following the storm, and their funerals had been held one day apart.

Nothing had been the same since then. Regardless of whether or not he dwelled on the event, or how many ships he built, life had become one steady, uphill climb.

The ghost—dressed in faded jeans, scuffed-up sneakers, and a yellow T-shirt that bore a cartoon dragon eating ice cream—wasn't a ghost, of course. But it took Garth a moment to realize this.

"You're Uncle Mike," he said, still holding on to the door.

His uncle grinned and held his hands out like a showman. "And you're Nephew Garth. Is there a door prize?"

No beard, Garth thought. *That's what's different. When he had his beard, it was hard to even tell they were twins.*

Not that he'd seen the guy too often; his dad and his uncle hadn't been very close. Four, maybe five times over the years, Uncle Mike had shown up out of the blue for a visit. And he'd come to the funeral, of course—arriving at the last minute, having driven from some other state.

"Well," Uncle Mike said, chuckling, "are you going to invite me in, or should I just . . . get lost?"

Garth snapped out of his trance and pulled the door

open wide. "No! Don't go—come in. Mom, it's Uncle Mike!"

His mom was standing at the entrance to the living room, the fingers of one hand touching her lips. She appeared to be in a trance of her own. Finally, she brought her hand away and said, "Mike . . . what in the world . . . I mean, what are you doing here?"

"Scaring the heck out of you two, apparently." He tapped a fist against Garth's shoulder and winked at him. Then he crossed the living room, opened his arms, and enfolded Garth's mom in a hug. "You look *great,* Sonja."

She hesitated a moment before returning the hug. "It's such a surprise seeing you, Mike. What brings you to Richmond?"

"I wish I could say business. It would mean I had something going on. But I'm between spots right now, on my way from one thing to another. You know me, I like to mix it up."

If there was any substance in that string of sentences, Garth couldn't pick up on it. He glanced at his mom to see if she'd understood, but she only asked, "Can I get you anything?"

"Some water would be great."

"Nothing to eat? We just finished dinner and there are leftovers—if you like meat loaf."

"That's really nice of you, but I stopped for a burger on the way into town. I'm good."

"I'll get you some water, then." She walked back into the kitchen.

Garth tried not to stare at this clean-shaven, near replica of his dad, but he couldn't help himself. Uncle Mike was dressed like a teenager. He had Garth's dad's straight, dark hair, but it was shaggy and scattered in a manner Jerry Rudd never would have worn it. He had his dad's nose and mouth, but the lopsided grin didn't match the wide, balanced smile Garth so clearly remembered his dad having. And yet the eyes . . . piercing, trusting, kind. They were his dad's eyes right down to the flecks of blue in the green.

Uncle Mike squatted down and patted the spaniel's head. "Hey, there, Starsky."

"That's Hutch," Garth told him. "Starsky died five years ago."

"Right, right. So how's the ol' schoolwork coming along?"

"It's summer."

"Good for you, then." Uncle Mike straightened up, pushed his hands down into his pockets, and rocked on his sneakers, gazing about the room.

He's wondering why we don't live in the house anymore, Garth thought. *He's thinking this place is pretty crappy.*

The apartment was the first floor of a chopped-up, three-story row house. There was an old water stain the shape of Texas on the living room ceiling that the landlord had been promising to have painted for months. The screen on the back door was held up on the outside with duct tape (feathered around the edges with dead moths). Half the windows didn't open; the other half opened but needed to be propped up with a stick. The place was a big step down from their old house, but it was all they could afford. Garth understood that, but he still felt a little embarrassed, watching his uncle eye the blemished ceiling.

As if he'd read his mind, Uncle Mike called out in a chipper, sincere-sounding voice, "Hey, these are nice new digs, Sonja."

"Oh," Garth's mom said, coming back in from the kitchen with his water. "They're okay. Please—sit down."

She handed him the glass and motioned toward the couch. He sank into it, crossed his long legs so that one ankle was perched on the opposite knee, and wobbled the sneakered foot that hung next to the coffee table. In a series of gulps that made his prominent Adam's apple rise and fall, he drank all of the water down.

"That may have been the best glass of water I've ever had," he said. Then he focused on Garth's mom.

"You really do look great, Sonja. Ever think about going back to modeling?"

She laughed gently. Garth couldn't remember the last time he'd heard her laugh. "You're remembering wrong. I never modeled, Mike. I wanted to when I was a teenager, but I didn't pursue it. I must have mentioned that to you once."

"Well, you could pick it up in a heartbeat, if you wanted to."

"Thank you."

Garth didn't think his mom looked so good. She'd seemed tired ever since she'd taken a second part-time job. There were almost always circles under her eyes, and she'd begun to slouch (something Garth didn't think she was even aware of, since she was the one who'd taught him that slouching made a poor impression).

Because he didn't want her to worry about giving him an allowance (she was already putting what little she could into the college fund he'd need in a couple of years), Garth had gotten his first job ever that summer. He worked at Peterson's, a downtown department store/cafeteria. But Mr. Peterson—a tightwad with a dandruff problem, and the only business owner Garth could find who was willing to hire someone under the age of sixteen—wouldn't pay him more than minimum wage and rarely gave him more than three shifts a week.

Uncle Mike was still wobbling his foot, still gazing around the room. What was *his* job? Garth wondered. He didn't even know where the man lived. His dad, who'd almost never said anything negative about anyone, had once referred to Mike as a "drifter." Another time, he'd called him a "lost soul." "He refuses to settle down," he'd said. "It's going to catch up with him one day."

"I'm glad you were listed in the phone book," Uncle Mike told his mom. "Otherwise, I might not have been able to find you."

"Well, you should have just called ahead. Our number didn't change."

"I wanted it to be a surprise. So . . . you just got tired of the house?"

She looked at the striped pattern of the wallpaper that was curling away in spots. "It was time to move," she said with determination. "Maybe it was because the house held too many memories. I don't know."

She *did* know, and so did Garth: the house held plenty of memories—most of them good ones—but the bank had taken it.

"That makes sense," Uncle Mike said. "Are you doing okay, though? In general?"

She took a deep breath that turned into a sigh as

it leaked out of her. "We take what comes, and make the most of what we have," she said, quoting her own motto for survival. "How about you? Are you still in Nevada?"

Nevada, Garth thought. *That's where he'd driven from when he came in for the funeral.*

Uncle Mike shook his head. "Nope, I haven't been there in over a year."

"Oh. Where are you living now?"

He shrugged as if the question made no difference. "Here and there. I don't like to be rooted in one spot."

She nodded her head, but seemed unclear as to how she should respond. After a moment, she said, "Isn't there a word for that?"

"There is. A beautiful word. *Wanderlust.* About the furthest I ever got from it was when I was engaged—did you know I was engaged once to this girl who lived in New York? But it didn't work out. In fact, it sort of became the *opposite* of wanderlust. There wasn't much lust, and all I wanted to do was wander." He chuckled.

Garth's mom cleared her throat. "So you came here from New York?"

"It's so good to see you guys," Uncle Mike said, shaking his head and reproducing his lopsided grin. "No, New York is ancient history. I came here from Houston—where I did pretty well. Enough to make me a happy camper for a while, anyway." He turned suddenly to Garth. "How about you? You're pretty quiet over there. How old are you now, Short Stuff, fourteen?"

"Fifteen," Garth said, feeling himself bristle at the nickname.

"Height's a sensitive subject around here," his mom informed Mike. "Somebody got himself into a fight over it at school this past year."

Uncle Mike cast Garth a wry look. "Is that right? So who won?"

"Me," Garth lied. If anything, he'd been on the verge of getting pulverized when Mr. Selgin, the assistant principal, pulled the two of them apart. Kevin Dougherty was half a foot taller than Garth and outweighed him by nearly twenty pounds.

"Good for you," Uncle Mike said.

"*Not* good for him," his mom countered, her eyes widening. "He had a black eye and a bloody elbow."

"Well." Mike scratched the dragon on his chest. "You've got to take up for yourself, let people know where you stand. Look at me: now *I* know what not to call you." He grinned at Garth.

"It's not funny," his mom said, raising her voice slightly. "He could get seriously hurt."

She was hinting at something else, Garth knew. He

12 •

said, "All right, Mom. Calm down."

But she only huffed as if he'd just told her go jump off a cliff. "I will calm down when the world gives me a reason to, young man."

She held his gaze for a challenging moment, then glanced toward Uncle Mike, who'd managed to erase the grin from his expression and raise his hands in a gesture of surrender.

They continued to "visit" into the evening. The concept had become foreign to Garth; ever since his dad had died and they'd moved into the apartment, they never had guests, let alone company. Was that what Uncle Mike was? Company? It was almost ten o'clock—hard to picture him getting back on the road at this late hour. It seemed to Garth that for as much talking as was going on, both Uncle Mike and his mom were skirting any *real* topics. Uncle Mike said very little about his current life but doled out plenty of compact little anecdotes about his past. ("Ever been to Buffalo? I spent a month there once trying to put something together— I don't recommend it." Then, a short while later: "I made it as far as California once. L.A. was crazy—just crazy—and San Francisco? Gorgeous, but not a lot going on.") Meanwhile, his mom didn't get into any specifics about how financially strapped they were, how hard she worked, or how things were so different for them now that his dad was gone. In fact, none of them had even *mentioned* his dad once the entire evening.

"So," Mike finally said, sinking down a bit lower into the couch, stretching his legs out beneath the coffee table, "I know I just dropped in out of the blue, but do you think it would be okay if I crashed here tonight? I'm a little road-weary, to tell you the truth. The couch is fine."

"Oh—" Garth's mom hesitated. She seemed somewhat uneasy about the idea. But then, she was a little uneasy about *everything*. "Of course," she said after a moment. "We have an extra room. It's small, but it has a daybed. Garth can make it up for you."

"That would be great. I really appreciate it."

"It's our pleasure," his mom said. Garth liked the idea that Mike would still be around in the morning, but then he heard his mother sniff, and when he looked at her again he saw that her eyes had suddenly teared up. "I'm sorry, Mike. It's just—without your beard, you really do look an awful lot like Jerry."

"Ah." Uncle Mike rubbed his jaw and nodded.

She got up then, and started into the kitchen to clean the dishes. Garth knew she was exhausted, so he said he would take care of it. She thanked him and told them both good night.

When she was gone from the room, Uncle Mike stood up and stretched, yawning. "I'm going to collect some stuff from my car," he said to Garth. "You can just point me to the sheets, if you want. I'll take care of myself."

"No, I can do it," Garth said. "The dishes won't take long."

"Aces," his uncle replied. "Be right back."

Garth let Hutch out into the backyard, then washed the dishes and stacked them in the dish strainer, occasionally peeking through the blinds of the kitchen window to where a sleek blue Camaro was parked along the curb next to their building. The car seemed to glow in the street light. Its trunk was open, and his uncle was bent over, rummaging around.

When he came back inside, he had a toiletry kit in one hand and a slim paperback book in the other. Some clothes were thrown over one arm.

Hutch barked impatiently at the back door.

"He sounds fierce," Mike said.

"He's gotten cranky in his old age." Garth let the dog in, and then led Mike to the guest room. Just across the hall from his own room, it was six by eight and had only one window, opening onto a skinny alleyway. Mike went into the bathroom and brushed his teeth while Garth made up the daybed. When he came back, Garth switched on the window fan and said, "Kind of a weird little room, huh?"

"It's perfect. Trust me, I'll sleep like a baby." Uncle Mike tossed the clothes onto a chair, and set his book on the little side table.

Garth peered at the book. "What are you reading?"

"*Double Indemnity.* They made a pretty good movie out of it about a million years ago. You should watch it sometime." His uncle glanced at the dull gray-avocado walls—the color of dust and mold, if you mixed the two together. "Hey"—he lowered his voice a notch—"you guys have had a rough time of it, haven't you?"

Lowering his own voice, Garth said, "It's been a pretty rotten year and a half."

"I know," his uncle told him. "For me, too, when I think about it."

How could you not think about it? Garth wondered.

"Your mom seems a little on edge."

"She's always been a worrier, but she's been worse since Dad died," Garth said. "Especially when it comes to me. It's like she's just waiting for something else bad to happen."

"Well, do you give her any reason to worry?"

She would say *yes*, he knew. But he and his mom saw certain things differently. And if Uncle Mike was only here for the night and would be gone tomorrow . . . there was no point in getting into personal stuff. "I don't think I do," he said.

"You seem like a stand-up guy to me."

Garth shrugged. "Thanks."

"Oh—and sorry about the 'short stuff' remark."

"It's okay. Night, Uncle Mike."

"Just 'Mike' is fine. Otherwise, I'll keep calling you 'Nephew Garth.'"

"Deal," Garth said. "Night, Mike."

"Good night."

He crossed the hall to his own room, and clicked on the light, thinking again how strange it was having someone else in their home. And not just anyone, but a near look-alike of his dad.

Hutch leaped up onto his bed and immediately closed his eyes. *Oh, to be a dog,* Garth thought. *To be able to fall asleep in a heartbeat and dream about squirrels and . . . Milkbones.* Maybe tonight—knowing Mike was right there, close by—his dad wouldn't feel quite so far away.

2

He woke in the morning to Hutch licking the side of his face.

"Yuck," he mumbled, turning away. "You need to brush your teeth."

But Hutch was more interested in rousing him, and Garth—an animal lover who could see himself becoming a vet one day—liked observing the dog's habits and behavior. Make one move in the morning, say one word, and that was it: in Hutch-think, you were officially awake and should get out of bed.

He was pulling on a T-shirt when he realized he hadn't had the nightmare the previous night. In fact, he'd had the opposite: a *good* dream about his dad— about the two of them painting the outside of the second hardware store his dad had opened several years ago. Cracking jokes. Sharing a can of soda. Basically just a good memory relived in his sleep. Why couldn't there be more dreams like *that*? He wondered if his uncle's presence had anything to do with it.

As he was coming down the hall, he heard his mom's voice and he paused to listen.

"And how long would you like to stay?"

"A couple of weeks," Mike said. "Maybe three? It would be great to spend some time with you guys under, you know, normal circumstances. A real treat for me. And I can help out with expenses—household stuff, groceries, that sort of thing. I wouldn't be a deadbeat, I promise."

Garth stayed where he was, still listening.

"Well, the thing is, Mike, you kept dodging me last night whenever I asked what you've been up to. If you're going to be under my roof, with Garth here—well, I'll just put this bluntly and hope I don't offend you: Are you dealing drugs?"

Garth nearly moaned with embarrassment. Only his mom would immediately let her mind go to such a worry.

But Mike didn't sound insulted or even surprised by the question. He told her no, then went on to explain that he didn't even smoke cigarettes or drink anymore, that he'd cleaned up his act a few years ago and had never felt better.

"Okay," she said. "Well, then, would you just tell me once and for all what it is you *do*? You've evaded that question ever since you walked through the door."

"You're right. Only because I didn't think you'd approve. Mostly, I gamble."

Garth thought of horse races, people jumping up and down and hollering—stuff he'd seen in movies—but his mother asked: "As in poker?"

"Poker, blackjack, even dice if I'm feeling lucky. And I have to say, I've got a knack for it. Most people don't think too highly of it, I know. But it's the life I lead. For right now, anyway."

Garth pictured Mike in a tux, à la James Bond, tossing a chip to the dealer. The image was almost laughable because Mike seemed so informal, so relaxed.

"But don't you have a degree in something? I remember you went to college."

"Yeah. Graphic design. And I took to it like a duck to water, but I didn't like working for a *company*, you know? It just felt gross, doing the same thing day after day. It felt like an anchor."

"Most jobs are."

"I guess so. I'll probably be heading for Atlantic City next, see if I can keep on my winning streak, but just so you know: I won't be doing any kind of gambling while I'm here."

"Good. That's a relief."

Mike asked her what she was doing these days,

workwise, and she told him about her two jobs (she was a secretary at a small law firm and a concierge at one of the nicer hotels). "Not very challenging work, and not very inspiring, either," she said.

Then the conversation shifted to Grandma Rudd in Ohio—how she was retired now, and how Mike tried to see her at least once a year. Garth's grandmother had a sweet, soft-sounding voice, and they used to drive up and spend Thanksgivings with her when his dad was still alive. They hadn't been able to do that last year because his mom couldn't get enough days off to make the trip. Besides, she'd told him, they couldn't really afford it. They'd settled for a long phone call after Thanksgiving dinner, in which his grandmother told him how proud of him she was, and how proud she knew his dad was, looking down from heaven.

"She's still waiting for me to give her a grandchild," Mike said with a small laugh.

Garth heard the creak of a chair and feared for a moment that his mom had gotten up and would catch him listening, but he heard her say, "Anyway, we'd be happy to have you stay with us for a little while."

"I really appreciate it," Mike said. "And like I said, I did pretty well in Houston, so whatever you need—a share of the rent, groceries—I can help out."

"Well, maybe," his mom said. "We'll see."

"This is like a dream come true for me, you know. A chance to finally get to know the two of you."

Finally. Garth was surprised at how happy he felt that Mike was going to stick around for a little while, but slightly annoyed by the implication that his dad had to be gone for it to happen. He cleared his throat, stepped around the corner, and emerged into the kitchen.

"Morning, sleepyhead," his mom said.

"Morning."

Mike was still in the dragon T-shirt but was wearing a pair of shorts and was barefoot. He had the *Richmond Times-Dispatch* open in front of him. He smiled at Garth. "How's it going, sport?"

Garth rubbed his eyes and sat down at the table.

The coffeepot was gurgling. His mom hummed softly as she stirred. When Mike turned a page of the newspaper, the combination of the three sounds brought back what felt like a previous life to Garth. He yawned and asked, "Can I have some coffee?"

"One cup," his mom said. "Only because it's Sunday."

"Sunday is coffee day?" Mike asked.

"For him it is. He asks for it all the time, but I don't want him to get hooked on it."

"I might turn into a junkie," Garth said. "Injecting it into my veins."

Mike sipped from his mug. "It *is* something of a habit."

He offered Garth the sports section, but Garth dug through the paper and pulled out the funny pages instead.

The waffles—complete with whipped cream and sliced strawberries—were served. Mike dug in. He seemed comfortable enough in their apartment to have lived there for years. "So," he said, leaning back in his chair and looking at Garth, "it looks like I'll be sticking around for a while."

"Really?"

"Yep." He dragged his napkin over his mouth. "Think you can put up with me?"

A short while later, Garth was sitting at his desk, gluing the bowsprit to a model of the HMS *Victory*, when he heard a knock. He anchored the bowsprit in place with a piece of Scotch tape to allow the glue to dry, then said, "Come in."

"Wow," Mike said, staring at the model as he entered the room. "That may be the most detailed thing I've ever seen in my life."

"It's about a seven on a scale of one to ten in terms of difficulty," Garth said. He was surprised at how impressed Mike seemed—and surprised at the little jolt of pride he felt, being able to impress.

"'The HMS *Victory*,'" Mike read off the front of the box, which Garth had cut out and taped to the wall over his desk as a visual guide. "It looks a little like the *Flying Dutchman*. Ever heard of that one?"

"I don't think so."

"It's a legendary ship whose crew was cursed to sail around the world helping other ships in distress forever and ever."

"Doesn't sound like such a bad curse."

"I guess the curse was in the 'forever' part." He gazed about the room at the dozens of ship models. "So you're a boat fanatic, like your dad?"

"No. I just build models."

"Well, you're good at it. I'd never have the patience for that kind of thing—unless there was some sort of shipbuilding contest and a big prize to be had." Mike sat down on the unmade bed and his eyes fell on the open closet, which was basically a landfill for dirty clothes and miscellaneous junk. Garth would have closed the door if he'd known he was going to have a visitor.

But Mike didn't seem to notice the mess. He was staring at the clothes rack. "What's with all the Halloween costumes?"

"Oh—I used to . . . reuse them." How humiliating:

the only reason he'd been able to reuse them was because he was still small enough to fit into them. "I don't dress up for Halloween anymore, obviously, but this guy at school told me I should keep them, said I could sell them on eBay one day and make a fortune."

"Good thinking," Mike said, eyeballing the half dozen polyester outfits, their hems a little frayed and their colors slightly faded. "Ever been to Duluth?"

"No. Why? Is that a good place to sell Halloween costumes?"

"Ha. No idea, but they've got this museum dedicated to ships. You might get a kick out of it."

Garth nodded. He took up one of the *Victory*'s hatch doors and ran sandpaper over the nub where he'd snapped it free of the plastic frame. He felt a little awkward, suddenly having an audience; he searched for something to say. "I'm glad you're staying," he finally managed. "It gets kind of boring around here in the summer."

"Don't you have friends around?"

Garth nodded. "My best friend, Lisa, lives just a few blocks over. And there are a few other people I hang out with who live nearby." The truth was that he'd practically become a hermit since the accident. Lisa was the only friend he hung out with now on a regular basis. "There's just, you know, not that much to do around here."

"I hear you. I was bored out of my mind when I was fifteen, and that was in a town a lot smaller than this. You just have to keep yourself occupied."

"Piggyback the neighbor's cable and I'll be occupied."

"Right. I'm taking you and your mom out for a fancy dinner tonight, by the way. If your calendar's open."

"I'm going to hang out with my friend Lisa this afternoon, but then I'm free."

"You don't sound so bored," Mike observed. "This Lisa—she your girlfriend?"

"Nope. Just a friend."

"Is she a hottie?"

The question nearly made Garth burst out laughing; Lisa *was*, in fact, hot. She had straight dark hair that often covered half her face in a shadowy, mysterious sort of way, and her body was long and sleek and tanned—but those weren't the sorts of things Garth went around noticing. His mind ran through a short list of possible responses as Mike smiled at him. "Yeah," he said, his nerve slipping. "She's a definite hottie."

It was Lisa who'd dubbed his predicament the Issue. She also called it the Big Duh and, every now and then, Project Garth. She was the first person that he'd come out to—nearly six months ago. Something about listening to her express her fear that the world would never embrace her for her art and her "creative vision" told him she'd have no problem with his sexual leanings. And she didn't. In fact, she claimed to have "intuited" his being gay from the first day they'd met, in the seventh grade. "I can read people like a book," she'd told him, "and your book screamed *gay* on page one." Though Garth was not "artistic" like Lisa, the two of them had a lot in common. They liked the same music, the same movies. They hated loud people and Hummer drivers and Republicans. And occasionally, to her great amusement, they liked the same guys—from afar, in Garth's case.

That afternoon, they lay stretched out on her bed side by side, listening to the latest Sufjan Stevens CD and ranking the songwriter's features. For Garth, Sufjan's eyes were the best thing about his looks, but Lisa disagreed. It was the *lips*, obviously, the *lips*. She'd thrown a red handkerchief over the lampshade on the nightstand, and it cast a pink hue onto the walls, where row after row of her photographs were taped up and curling in the humidity. Most of them— black-and-white, shot digitally, and Photoshopped with swaths of color—were of strangers captured in random moments: a man with a parakeet on his shoulder waiting for the bus; an old woman sitting on a bench in Capitol Square, transfixed by a pigeon; a young girl watching a Civil War reenactment at the base of the Robert E. Lee Memorial. Lisa was calling the series "Obfuscation" (whatever that meant).

"So, my uncle's in town," Garth said, gazing up at her ceiling, where some long-dead, bald-headed painter gazed back from a postcard. "He showed up last night out of the blue."

"What uncle?"

"Mike. My dad's brother."

"Oh, yeah," she said, and then, "Shh! Listen to this part."

Sufjan's breathy voice dissolved into one prolonged, slowly fading note from his trumpet.

"Perfection," she said. "I remember your uncle from the funeral. He had that scruffy beard, and it trembled when he cried."

That day was something of a blur in Garth's mind. He remembered just a few specific—and significant—details (the shine on the casket; the feeling of his mom's wedding ring as he held her hand; the feeling of his other hand being squeezed by Lisa, who stayed by his side the entire afternoon).

"The beard's gone now," he said.

"Yikes. That must be like looking at a clone of your dad."

"I think it was a little weirder for my mom than it was for me—but you get used to it pretty fast."

"So what's he like?"

Garth thought about how best to describe Mike. Laid-back? Easygoing? "He's like a big teenager," he said. "Ish. I mean, he's this middle-aged guy, obviously, but he doesn't *seem* like one."

He was in the middle of telling her about the conversation he'd overheard that morning when Lisa interrupted him, midsentence.

"Hold on. Your uncle *gambles* for a living?"

"That's what he said."

"And his mom—your grandmother—doesn't have a problem with that?"

"I don't think so. She might not even know about it, though."

"Why can't I have parents like that? I mean, look at me. I've got talent, I've got genius, and all my parents do is tell me I'll starve if I pursue a life as a photographer. They're shelling out for my idiot brother to major in failing at VCU, and they're smothering my creative aspirations!"

"I was talking about my uncle," he reminded her.

"Sorry. Go on."

"Anyway, it looks like he's going to be staying with us for a while."

"Do you think he's going to run a poker game out of your apartment?"

"The spare room's the size of a closet."

"I was kidding. You never know, though—he might get the itch and want to stir up a little action. If you smell cigar smoke and hear 'Come to Papa!' you'll know."

"Freak," he said.

"*You're* the freak. You get to kiss any part of Sufjan, and you pick his eyes? Please."

"You didn't say anything about kissing! You just asked what my favorite part was. It doesn't make any difference anyway. He's straight, and I'm . . ."

"Crooked?"

"Chained up. Censored. Stifled."

"Speaking of which." Lisa propped herself up on an elbow to look at him, her thin eyebrows raised. "Any new developments on the Issue?"

He groaned. "No. Project Garth is still dead in the water."

"How long has it been now? Two months?"

"Three months, one week, five days," he muttered. "And counting."

His mom was the second person he'd come out to, after things had gone so smoothly with Lisa. He didn't like hiding what was beginning to feel like such a large part of himself from her. In fact, *not* telling her, he decided, was like watering the seed of a beanstalk—one that would grow fat and tall, given the chance, and one he might eventually use to climb away from her, emotionally. He didn't want that. At this point, they only had each other.

He planned out what he would say, and he ran through possible reactions in his head. He couldn't picture her screaming, "No, no, no!" any more than he could picture her throwing her arms around him and exclaiming, "How wonderful!" Just thinking about it was tiring.

He finally eased them into the topic one night during dinner. He was careful to say first that he had something very important to tell her. He clarified that nothing was *wrong*, that everything was *fine*. Then he made his announcement.

Just two words, but still. Two phenomenally important words, when you stuck them together.

She, the Queen of Trepidation, remained silent.

"It's not a phase, and it's not some confusion on my part," he said, the speech practically scripted because he'd rehearsed it so much. "I'm not still figuring it out; I *know* it. It's what I am, and I've been wanting to tell you."

"Garth," she finally said, frowning down at her plate. She drew in a breath, held it a moment, then exhaled and looked him in the eye. "Let's talk about this later, okay?"

For all the possible reactions he'd run through his mind, he hadn't expected that one.

"Can you do me that favor?" she asked. "Can we just put this topic on hold?"

"Sure," he muttered, wondering exactly what she meant by "on hold."

Thus commenced the waiting. Hours of it. Then days. A long, awkward week that bled into another.

When he brought it up again, ten days later—over breakfast this time (he thought it might be a better strategy to catch her when she wasn't exhausted from a day's work)—she came back with the same response: "We agreed to put that topic on hold."

"But what does that mean? On hold till when?"

"Until you're older and more capable of dealing with it. Until you're seventeen—or even eighteen. Between then and now, I think it's best to just shelve the issue."

"*Shelve* it?" he asked, trying to control his tone. "How?"

"By not doing anything about it. By not *telling* anyone."

"I just told you."

"Outside the family," she clarified. "Please, Garth.

I've got nothing against gay people. You know me. But the world is a dangerous place."

"Is it because you think I couldn't defend myself, if someone tried to gay-bash me?" he asked.

He could tell by her expression that that was exactly what it was—or at least part of it (though, truth be told, she'd probably be just as worried about him if he were six feet two). She fumbled for a moment, searching for words, then said, "The fact is, there are many deceitful, harmful people out there, and you never know who you're getting involved with when you start trusting them. I couldn't bear it if something happened to you. I couldn't. It would kill me."

"This isn't fair," he said. "You're making it all about you."

"The *world* isn't fair, Garth. That's why we have to make careful, sensible decisions—even if they aren't ideal. Promise me you'll keep this private until you're older and more equipped to take care of yourself."

There was no changing her mind, he knew. And there was no telling her now that he'd already come out to Lisa. "Fine," he said, wondering whether or not he'd be able to keep such a huge promise.

The next time he saw Lisa was at Bone Sweet Bone, the dog rescue shelter where they both volunteered on Wednesday afternoons. He recounted the whole

• 33

frustrating conversation and, with utter embarrassment, asked her not to tell anyone else and to pretend she herself didn't know, if anyone asked.

"This is major," she said, wiping out a cage. "I mean, how are you going to have any gay friends? Much less a boyfriend?"

"I know, I know." He hoisted a bag of dog food down from a shelf. When it hit the floor, half the dogs started whimpering. One of them let out a high-pitched bark. "*Quiet,*" he told the dog, "or you won't get lunch."

"Nice vet you're going to make."

"He knows I'm kidding. Don't you . . ." He squinted at the index card taped to the cage, which bore the temporary name that Ms. Kessler, the shelter's owner, had given the dog, ". . . Toodles. Anyway, I keep hoping she'll come around, once she's had time to digest it. But I'm not crossing my fingers."

"You should call ROSMY."

"Who?"

"It's not a who; it's a hotline. The Richmond Organization for Sexual Minority Youth. Friends of mine have used them before and said they were really helpful."

"What do they do, teach you how to be gay?"

"They counsel. They offer advice."

He cut the string on the dog food bag and tore it

open. "I want the program that fast-tracks me to eighteen, so I can start being myself."

"You know," she said, "you could call anonymously, make up a name. You could be . . . Todd."

"Or Toodles."

"'Hello, ROSMY? This is Toodles J. Homosex on the line, and I have a few questions for you.'"

"Shut up!" He laughed and threw a nugget of dog food at her.

"Anyway. There it is. Consider it. Anonymity can be a wonderful thing."

He pondered the idea for another few days. Then, while his mom was at work, he looked up the number and dialed it from the wall phone in the kitchen.

A man answered, identifying himself as a counselor. He was halfway through asking how he could help when Garth hung up on him.

Wimp, he thought. *What's the big deal?* It was as if he'd been infected with his mom's worries, her panic, her fear. The idea infuriated him, so he picked up the phone and dialed again.

The same voice answered, the same greeting.

"Hi, um, my name is . . . Greg? And I'm just wondering if I can get some advice." There was a tremble in his voice he couldn't suppress. He felt as if he'd just realized he was gay five minutes ago.

But as the person on the other end of the line—calmly, reassuringly—began asking him a few questions and then actually *listened* to what he had to say, he realized that talking to a stranger had extreme benefits. Lisa was right: anonymity *was* a wonderful thing. He told the counselor he was gay; he told him about Lisa; he told him about coming out to his mom, and her reaction. Then it dawned on him that in order for any of this to make sense, he would have to talk about his dad. He did. And he surprised himself by not crying. Halfway through his monologue, he noticed that the tremble was gone from his voice. He didn't even feel nervous anymore.

"So, Greg," the man said—and like some soothing, otherworldly entity, he began to offer small bits of advice. A few questions, too, but mostly advice. Suggestions. Options. Nothing drastic and nothing derogatory about his mom and her position. The organization held in-person counseling sessions, the man explained. "Greg" could come in with his mom and speak with someone who could help them understand each other's points of view more clearly. Did he think his mom would be willing to come in with him for an appointment?

"I doubt it," Garth said. "But I can ask."

He hung up feeling a few notches better.

But his mom's reaction to the news that he'd called was worse than ever. She was practically furious. "If you respect me," she said, "you'll stick to your promise."

If he *respected* her? Of course he respected her. But did she respect him and who he was becoming? Was she even capable of it, buried under so many blankets of fear and distress? It seemed he could only reach a certain part of her anymore. That basic, functioning-human part: *Let's eat breakfast, See you tonight, What's for dinner? Love you, Sleep well.* Mourning and missing his dad had dominated their lives since the accident; that made sense to him. But did that mean they had to just shut down in their current state?

Lisa was now hanging off the bed, one of her long, sinewy arms stretching to her desk so she could fiddle with her iTunes. Sufjan segued into Belle and Sebastian.

"Any chance this uncle of yours is a member of The Big Duh society?" she asked.

"God, wouldn't *that* flip my mom out? I don't think he is, though. I mean, he's not married, but he said he was engaged once and he definitely gives off a straight . . . vibe."

"Too bad. It might have been a chance to shake things up. You know—make her face Project Garth."

Garth rolled over onto his stomach and folded his

hands beneath his chin. "She faces it every time she looks at me," he said. "Only she doesn't see it."

His mom had apparently endured all the shaking up that she could handle for a while. She clearly didn't need him rocking the boat.

Bad metaphor, he thought.

Three months. One week. Five days.

And counting.

Mike made Garth's mom choose the restaurant for dinner that night. She tried to get away with picking a few less-expensive places that were nearby, but Mike looked up the reviews on Garth's computer, and told her she had to aim higher. Finally, she picked The Tobacco Company, a restaurant in an old tobacco warehouse in Shockoe Bottom that she assured him was "fancy." "We're there," Mike said.

Garth's mom put on a dress and pinned her hair up in a way that made her look younger and much less tired (though that might have been due to the makeup). Mike wore a white button-down shirt and slacks, a striped tie, and a slightly rumpled blazer. "Oh, go put on a tie," Garth's mom said when Garth emerged from his room in a dress shirt and trousers.

"It's just dinner," he protested.

She pointed to the back of the apartment. He did an

about-face and returned to his room.

He only owned two ties. One had been a gift from Lisa and had Charlie Chaplin on it; he doubted his mom would approve. The other was deep blue and speckled with tiny red dots. He drooped it around his neck and stood in front of the mirror trying over and over again to get the knot right, but his dad had always been the one to tie his tie for him. He'd stand behind him in front of the mirror and look at Garth's face in the reflection, his hands moving effortlessly while he talked about something else. Who had tied Garth's tie for the funeral? A neighbor? He couldn't remember.

"You about ready?" Mike asked, peering through the open door.

"No," Garth said. "I don't think I'll ever know how to work one of these stupid things."

Mike walked into the room and stepped up behind him. He put his arms around Garth's shoulders, taking hold of both ends of the tie. Looking Garth's reflection in the eye, he said, "Watch my hands and learn." The hands started swimming. "I didn't think I'd ever understand poker the first time I walked into a casino. That was on a cruise ship, of all places. First and last cruise I ever went on. Just a big, floating hotel. I was playing this sunburned grill salesman from Saint Claire who wouldn't shut up about grills. I just kept looking at my cards and thinking, Some of these look pretty good together. I'll stick with them. Then I drew the two of clubs and the six of diamonds, and that looked like a nice collection, so while he yammered on, I just sat tight. When the time came, the dealer had two pair and the grill salesman got this big, cheesy grin on his face and showed us a straight. 'Whatcha got?' he asked, and I laid down my cards. And you know what?"

He removed his hands. The knot was clean, the length perfect—just long enough to cover Garth's belt buckle.

"I learned that day that a full house beats a straight," Mike said to his reflection, smiling. "Look at you. A ladies' man if I ever saw one."

At the restaurant they sat beneath myriad stained-glass ceiling lamps, beside an exposed-brick wall divided by ancient beams. Garth's mom said for maybe the fourth time how nice it was that Mike was treating them, and he encouraged her—and Garth—to "order large." She ordered a salad and her favorite food: scallops. Garth ordered a shrimp cocktail and, at Mike's prodding, a steak. Mike had the same. He told more stories about his past during the meal; he mimicked the voices of the characters he'd encountered, his hands and face animated, and piled one anecdote on top of another. Garth's mom seemed to loosen up, and laughed more than he'd seen her laugh in a long time. It made him even more glad that Mike was going to stick around for a little while. They left the restaurant stuffed and happy. Strolling down the cobblestone streets of Shockoe Bottom with his tie expertly knotted around his neck, Garth felt like someone other than himself. Or maybe he just felt *happy* for the first time in a long while.

"I have a surprise for you guys," Mike said as they were pulling up in front of the apartment in his mom's station wagon. "It's in my car. I'll meet you in a sec."

Garth and his mom went inside, sat in the living room, and waited. When Mike came in, he was holding a shoe box with a rubber band around it.

"I've had these for years. They're of me and Jerry. I thought you might like to have them." He sat in the armchair next to the couch and handed Garth's mom the box.

"Oh, Mike," she said, "are you sure?"

"I have more. You guys should have these."

"Well—thank you." She took the rubber band off, lifted the lid, and began sifting through the snapshots, passing them to Garth one at a time. "They're wonderful. I have maybe one picture from Jerry's childhood. I think it's of him on a swing set, wearing striped pants."

"I remember that swing set," Mike said. "We got it for our fourth birthday."

"These really are priceless." She handed snapshot after snapshot to Garth, who collected them all in his lap, absorbing the images. How strange to see his grandmother slim and smooth-skinned and dark haired. Stranger, still, to see so many pictures of the two interchangeable boys. As they neared the bottom of the box, Garth was conscious of the fact that there wasn't a single picture of them together in adulthood. The most recent photo was of the two of them standing side by side at what looked to be a carnival. They weren't boys, but they weren't quite men yet, either. Maybe seniors in high school. Garth could easily tell them apart at that age, even though they were "identical." His dad was on the left, his arms folded across his chest. Mike was on the right, hands buried in his pockets. Neither one of them was smiling. If it weren't for the fact that they were twins, they might have looked like two strangers in a crowd.

3

The next morning, after Garth's mom left for work, Mike continued to make himself at home. He poured himself a bowl of cereal and spent a couple of hours on the couch with his feet up on the coffee table, clicking through the four television stations they got with what seemed to be a sense of curiosity rather than a need for entertainment—as if he were observing an entirely new culture. "Who's the guy on the horse?" he asked while he was watching the local news. "They keep cutting to that same statue before they go to a commercial."

Garth was just coming back into the room, his arms filled with dirty laundry—the next item on his list of chores. It almost felt as if he had a lazy older brother in the house rather than an uncle—but he was happy that Mike felt comfortable here, and glad for the company. "That's Robert E. Lee."

"Really? What's he, the town mascot?"

"Pretty much."

"I would have thought that'd be what's-his-name. The Lincoln counterpart."

"Jefferson Davis?"

"Him," Mike said.

Garth shrugged. "He's got a statue, too. A couple of them. But Lee's is bigger."

"It's all about size," Mike said.

Garth carried the laundry into the kitchen, where the stacked washer/dryer unit was tucked into a tiny closet. He'd just turned on the washing machine—it rattled like an old boiler against the confines of the surrounding walls—when the phone rang.

"Hello?"

"Okay, so my mom isn't devoting *all* her energy to telling me I'll never make a dime off my art, and for the first time in my life I'm thankful to have a dumb hick for a brother."

"Hi, Lisa."

"Jason got his girlfriend pregnant!"

"*What?*"

"Yep. He can waste a year in college and end up with only six credits and they don't bat an eye, but *this*, my friend, has rocked the house."

"What's he going to do?"

"Well, he actually *wants* to 'settle down.' As in get married, get a job at a gas station or whatever, and become a dad. But my parents are hinting around at a whole nother course of action."

"Meaning . . ."

"One guess, Einstein."

"They suggested it outright?"

"Suggested it? They offered to pay for it!"

"Well, what about his girlfriend? Doesn't *Stacey* have a say in this? It's her body, after all."

"That's what I told my parents! I got that leave-the-room look they give me whenever the crisis is about Jason and not me. God forbid we ever both get into trouble at the same time."

"When have you ever been in trouble?"

"Hello? Last summer? The Nude Descending the Monkey Bars shoot I did of Taylor Markson?"

"Oh, yeah. I'm still waiting for my copies of that, by the way."

"Won't happen. Taylor made me promise, and my parents confiscated the negatives. Anyway, it'll be interesting to see how this whole thing plays out, because I don't think Stacy's that into Jason, but I think she *is* into keeping the baby. So what's up with you?"

"Not much. Chores, mainly."

"Are we still going to hang out at my place this afternoon?"

"Definitely. I'll call before I come over."

"I'll be the one *without* the pregnant girlfriend."

They hung up, and he rechecked his list. He'd saved

the worst for last: the hedges. The front and back yards of the house were shared by all the tenants, but the landlord shaved thirty dollars off the rent for Garth to take care of basic outside maintenance, including the grass and the hedges. The grass was easy, just a few swipes with the mower, since there was almost no yard to speak of. But the hedges that lined both sides of the yard were a pain—especially in the dead heat of summer. He descended into the musky, cobwebbed basement and took the hedge clippers from the nail next to the fuse box. He was coming back up when he heard Mike's voice through the kitchen window: "You've got nothing to worry about, Stu. I talked to Marty, and he's going to have a money order in the mail within a month. Well, that was the arrangement made between Marty and Phil, so maybe you should talk to Marty yourself. He seemed fine with it, last I heard. Yeah. Talk to him. Talk to *Phil,* if you want. I'm sticking to what we agreed on. All right. Yeah, yeah, I got it. Later."

Garth hesitated next to the window and peeked in. His uncle was punching another number into his cell phone.

"Marty? It's Mike. . . . Mike Rudd, who do you think? . . . It doesn't *matter* where I am. Listen, you know that juggling we talked about? Does Phil know about it? Well, you might want to do some fast footwork because Stu's going to be calling you, and if he can't get hold of you, there's a good chance he's going to be calling Phil directly. . . . Hey, the juggle was *your* idea. . . . Yes, it was. . . . Well, maybe my memory's better than yours. Anyway, I'm out of the loop at this stage—well, I'm *practically* out of the loop. You know what I mean. The point is, you should be expecting a call from Stu and you might want to head it off at the pass. Listen, I've got to go. I'll be in touch, okay?"

Mike sounded more like a loan shark than a gambler. Garth was curious but thought it best not to ask. He ducked under the window and carried the clippers out into the yard.

He'd worked three-quarters of the way around the perimeter when Mike stepped outside. The screen fell away as he pushed open the door. "Whoa!" he said, catching it with one hand.

"Sorry," Garth called from across the yard. "It does that. The tape is old."

"It needs one of those . . . what's it called?"

"A new door?"

"Ha—no, I mean one of those . . . things to fix it with. Rubber piping and a whatsit." He pushed at the tape until the screen was back in place, then crossed the yard to where Garth was clipping. Hutch lay stretched out on the grass nearby. Mike reached down and

picked up a ratty tennis ball—one of Hutch's toys—
and waved it at the dog. He tossed it across the yard
into the dead garden, and the spaniel got up, lumbered
over, and retrieved it, but didn't bring it back. "You're
working up a sweat, there."

"We get a discount on the rent if I do this," Garth
explained, wiping a hand over his brow. "I mow the
lawn, too."

"Here," Mike said, "let me take over for a while."

"You don't have to do that. I'm almost done."

But Mike insisted, and took the clippers out of his
hands. He clipped with a flair—one or two branches at
a time. Even so, he seemed to move along at a pace that
at least matched if not surpassed Garth's. "Your mom
tells me money's been pretty tight lately."

"Yeah. That's why I took my job—so she wouldn't
have to shell out spending money for me. I'm trying
to save a little of what I'm making, too. You know, for
emergencies. Mom already works two jobs," Garth
said.

"There are ways outside the . . . traditional chan-
nels to make a buck." He continued to work the clippers across the last hedge.

Garth moved along with him, his hands in his
pockets. "What, like rob a bank?"

"No!" Mike laughed. "I'm just talking about less

traditional, more creative ways to generate income."
Finished, he stepped back and eyeballed the hedge with
his thumb raised before his eyes, as if gazing at a painting in progress. "Rob a bank," he repeated, chuckling.
"That's a good one. What do you say we rake this stuff
up and make some lunch?"

Hutch knew the word *lunch*. He let go of the tennis
ball and started for the house.

There was bread in the cabinet. Bologna and American cheese and mayo in the fridge. Garth pulled all
these out and laid them on the counter, then got down
two plates.

"Hold that thought," Mike said, washing his hands
in the sink and eyeing the food. "Let's explore."

Garth was pretty certain there was nothing to explore in their kitchen. But he let Mike go at it while he
moved the clothes from the washer to the dryer.

Mike went through each of the cabinets and
plumbed the depths of the refrigerator. He found a
box of pasta shells and set a pot of water on the stove.
As the shells cooked, he stirred up the contents of two
cans of tuna fish, some chopped olives, and a tomato.
He discovered a block of Parmesan cheese and a cheese
grater Garth didn't even know they owned. Canned
asparagus. Sweet pickles. It seemed to take no time at

all to prepare, and yet there it was: a lunch that could have been served in a restaurant. "Let's eat in the living room," Mike suggested. "That dryer's turned the kitchen into a sauna."

They set their plates on the coffee table and sat on the carpet on either side of it. Hutch positioned himself between them. When Mike set one of his pickles on the table in front of Hutch's snout, the dog gobbled it up.

Garth took a swig of soda. "What sort of graphic design do you know? Web pages?"

"How'd you know I did graphic design?"

Oops. He'd learned that eavesdropping. He cleared his throat and said, "Mom told me. So is it mainly Web page stuff?"

"Sad truth of it is the technology's probably left me behind now. I don't know why I got the degree; I'm never going to chain myself to a company. Not that knowing the basics doesn't come in handy now and then." He pointed across the coffee table at Garth in a mock-dramatic way. "And not that education isn't important."

"Yeah, yeah," Garth said. He knew that was true, but at the same time he admired Mike's take on life, how he lived it exactly the way he wanted to, despite the "norm"—the very qualities Garth's dad hadn't approved of. But maybe his dad never really got to know Mike as an adult.

"How about you?"

"What do you mean?"

"What do you like to do—besides build boat models? Go to movies? Read? Fight the girls off with a stick?"

Garth hesitated, mid-chew. "I don't fight them off with a stick."

"A good-looking guy like you? Come on. You've got the Rudd genes. *You* might have twins, you know."

"You think?"

Mike nodded. "They tend to skip a generation, and you're the generation that got skipped." He stuffed a forkful of pasta into his mouth. "Oh, I get it. You don't fight the girls off; you let them have you. Smart man."

Family, Garth thought. *He's family. If I tell him I'm not breaking the promise, right?*

Mike *seemed* worldly enough not to flip out about it. Plus, he couldn't bear the thought of two, possibly three weeks with his uncle in the house making the same occasional, straight nudge-nudge remarks he had to endure at school. He took a swallow of soda so enormous it burned his throat and said, "I don't plan on having kids, actually."

"No? Bachelor for life, like me?"

"I'm not into girls."

He saw the grin leave his uncle's mouth for just a moment. Mike studied him, narrowing his eyes, as if reassessing him as a person. Then, slowly, the grin returned and he began to nod his head yes. "All right," he said. "That's cool. I like somebody who . . . knows what he likes."

"Really? You're okay with it?"

Mike shrugged. "Why wouldn't I be? I have gay friends."

"You *do*?"

He laughed. "We're talking about people, not Martians. What is it, nine, ten percent of the world is gay? Probably more than that, if truth be told. Of course I have gay friends. *You've* got gay friends, right?"

Garth felt his face redden. "Actually, I don't. My friend Lisa does, though."

"Well, why aren't her friends your friends?"

"Because . . . "

"You're not out to her."

"No, it's not that." Suddenly, the topic felt too complicated to articulate, even though he thought about it all the time. He was beginning to doubt whether or not he should have said anything. What was that phrase Mr. Mosier had used in chemistry class? *In for a penny, in for a pound.* "Lisa knows. But then I told Mom, and she freaked out and made me promise not to tell anyone else. Outside the family, I mean. So you don't count. But then I couldn't tell her I told Lisa, and I had to tell Lisa not to tell anyone. It's kind of a mess."

"Wait—your mom freaked out that you're gay?"

"She's just . . . hyperworried I'll get beaten up or something." He went on to give his uncle a condensed version of the argument they'd had.

Mike took it all in with a puzzled look on his face. "How can someone be expected to 'shelve' his sexuality for three years? Someone who isn't confused, that is."

Garth felt a wave of relief wash over him. Mike's reaction was the same as Lisa's had been, but it was different—and good—to hear it from an adult. And a relative, no less. It almost felt like he was hearing it from his dad.

"You never told your dad, did you?" Mike asked, reading his mind again.

Garth shook his head.

"I wonder how your mom would have reacted if your dad was here. Obviously, part of her reaction is the fact that she's still dealing with the accident. She's grieving, I get that. But I also wonder how she might have dealt with your . . . announcement . . . if she had another person—your dad—here to talk about it with."

"Yeah," Garth said.

"Hey." Mike reached across the coffee table and tapped Garth's shoulder. "I'm glad you told me."

"Really?"

"You confided in me. I take that as a compliment. Thanks."

Garth couldn't help but smile. "You're welcome."

A little while later, Mike tapped on the door to Garth's room and asked him if they had a toolbox. They'd had several—his dad had been quite a tool collector, having owned two different hardware stores—but the toolboxes were in storage. The walk-in unit his mom had rented was like a microcosm of their former life. It was stacked with furniture from their old house that wouldn't fit in the apartment, crammed with cartons of knickknacks and lamps, and, worst of all, filled with box after box of his dad's shirts, pants, and shoes (his mom had eventually brought herself to clean out the closet, but hadn't been able to give the clothes away). Garth had been in the storage unit only once since they'd filled it, and walking into that dank, crowded square of corrugated steel had felt like entering a tomb. An extension of his dad's grave.

"The storage place is way far away. It takes, like, an hour to get there," he exaggerated. "Why? What do you need? We've got a hammer and a couple of screw-drivers here."

"A bit more than that. Tell you what—do feel like going for a drive? We can go to a hardware store, pick up what I need, and then you can give me a mini-tour of Richmond."

"Sure," Garth said. "Oh, wait. I sort of told my friend Lisa I'd hang out with her this afternoon."

Mike shrugged. "Bring her along. You guys can tag-team tour-guide."

When Garth called Lisa, she sounded less than en-thusiastic. "I thought you were going to be over here by now. I have this new CD I want to play you—a Brit-ish import of a band called Kazooster. I've listened to it fifty-four times in the past two days; it's amazing."

"Sorry, I—I just had all these chores. Why don't we do the mini-tour first and hang out later? Mike says we can swing by and pick you up."

"'Mike'? You're not calling him 'Uncle Mike'?"

"He doesn't want me to."

"Oh. Well, I guess Kazooster can wait."

The sharp blue Camaro was, by far, the coolest car Garth had ever been in. He rode shotgun; Mike steered with his right hand and hung his left arm out the win-dow. In Lisa's driveway, he did his shave-and-a-haircut tap on the horn.

She came out a minute later, her camera hanging around her neck.

"She's going to take pictures of us?" Mike asked.

"No. It's her thing, though. Photography. She rarely goes anywhere without her camera." Garth opened his door and leaned forward so she could climb into the backseat, but Mike put the car in park, left it idling, and got out to officially meet her. "I'm Mike," he said, extending his hand.

She seemed caught off guard by the formality. "Lisa," she said, and shook the hand.

"Lisa, it's a pleasure to meet you. And clearly it was destined to happen, because of our shirts."

Garth peered through the windshield—they were both wearing Pink Floyd T-shirts. Lisa's was fairly new, the decal deliberately scuffed up to make it look old; Mike's *was* old, and falling apart, right down to the collar that was separating from the shirt in places.

"*Dark Side of the Moon* is awesome," she said.

"I couldn't agree more."

Garth waved her over, and she climbed in.

"So you're a photographer?" Mike asked, glancing at her in the rearview mirror as he pulled away from her house.

"I'm an artist," she replied.

"Good for you," Mike said. "I'm not, but people

like me need people like you to open our eyes to the world, you know? Most of us go through life in a . . . vacuum. When, really, there's amazing stuff happening all around us—and not just beautiful stuff, but horrible, twisted, or sometimes achingly mundane stuff. A million missed moments every day, because we can't *see* them. Artists help us do that. Particularly photographers, who deal with such concrete subjects. They help fill that void."

Garth himself couldn't have scripted a statement that would have pleased Lisa more. It was as if Mike had been coached on the subject of *her* and was giving his oral exam. He turned around and glanced at Lisa in the backseat. She was nodding her head slowly and appeared a little stunned. After a moment she said, simply, "Yeah."

"So where's this hardware store?" Mike asked.

"Turn here. We'll go to one on Broad Street," Garth said. The last store his dad had owned had been across the James River, on the south side of town. It was a greeting card and party supply store now. He hadn't been inside but had ridden past it with his mom once; neither one of them had remarked on it as they'd passed.

Mike told them he'd only be a minute, and disappeared into the Broad Street store.

"So," Garth said when they were alone. "What do you think?"

"About what?"

"My uncle."

"I think it's completely spooky how much he looks like your dad. How can you stand it?"

"The more I'm around him, the more I can see little differences. I don't even know what they are, but I see them."

"His personality's a lot different from your dad's."

"How do you mean?"

"Well, your dad was a salesman, right? He had a store; he sold things."

"So?"

"But he didn't *talk* like a salesman."

"And Mike does?"

"I don't know yet. I'm still getting a read on him. He seems a little . . . slick."

"Give him a chance," Garth said. He liked Mike, and he wanted Lisa to like him. After all, they were the only two people he could truly be himself around.

Before long, Mike emerged with a bag in each hand. He put the bags in the trunk, then got back in behind the wheel.

"What's all that?" Garth asked.

"Necessaries," he said. "So—where to now? We

don't have to get out of the car; you can just point out the good stuff."

"That may be a challenge," Lisa muttered.

At Garth's suggestion, they made their way downtown to Capitol Square. They showed him the Capitol Building and the surrounding grounds, the governor's mansion, the conglomerate statue of various American icons topped by George Washington. From there, they directed Mike past the grand Jefferson Hotel, and finally they cut back over so that he could drive down Monument Avenue—a wide, brick thoroughfare with a tree-lined median and stately houses lining either side.

"The pride and joy of Richmond," Lisa droned from the backseat.

They rounded the monument to J.E.B. Stuart, his horse reared up as if a mouse had startled it.

"He was one of the head honchos?" Mike asked.

"He was a general," Garth said. "Kind of stubborn. I think I read that somewhere, or saw it in a documentary."

They carried on, and soon came to the traffic circle surrounding the massive monument to Robert E. Lee.

"The guy from the news!" Mike said, leaning sideways to get a look at the statue.

"Yep. Facing south, because if he were facing *north,*

the earth would crack in half or something."

"What a strange place this must have been—maybe still is," Mike said. "I mean, look at him. How high up he is on that marble base. The people who erected that must have revered him like some kind of god."

"God of the racists," Lisa offered.

Mike grinned and glanced at Garth.

"We sort of get the Civil War stuff shoved down our throats around here," Garth told him.

"That makes sense, given the location."

"Yeah, but the whole what-it-stands-for thing is just kind of . . . depressing."

"It's sickening, is what it is," Lisa said. "I mean, what are they celebrating, anyway? Southern pride? Pride in what? Losing the fight to keep *slavery* alive?"

"Hindsight is not always twenty-twenty," Mike said. "Sometimes people look back at a situation, and they still don't get it."

"Not only that; they stage reenactments of what few battles they won!" Lisa said. "I mean, how pathetic."

"Who's that?" Mike asked, pointing up ahead.

"Jefferson Davis," Garth said. Davis—a somewhat gaunt, unbearded man—stood atop a column, flanked by a semicircle of other, taller columns.

"Why doesn't he get a horse?"

"Because he was the president. He wasn't in battle."

"Ah," Mike said. "Like most politicians. They should have cast him in bronze behind his desk, with a cup of tea in his hand."

They crossed the Boulevard and rounded the monument to Stonewall Jackson.

"How come all the horses are in different positions?" Mike asked.

"It means how they died—in battle, or afterward, or whatever."

"It means he was a big racist pig who killed a lot of people," Lisa groaned.

"You should work for the bureau of tourism," Mike said, grinning at her in the rearview mirror. "You could give the anti-Richmond tour."

"Any day," she said. "I mean, it's not the worst place in the world, but this Civil War stuff is just morose."

"Well, what else is there to look at?" Garth asked her. "Want to drive out onto the interstate and gawk at the Philip Morris plant?"

"No, thank you," she said. "I'll suffer my ancestors' past with utter humility, like any other intelligent twenty-first-century person."

"Jackson had to have his arm sawed off in a tent hospital," Garth said, turning back to his uncle. "When I was in the eighth grade, we took a field trip to the Museum of the Confederacy, and they have his uniform in a glass case—*and* the saw they used to cut off his arm!"

"Do they have the arm?" Mike asked.

Lisa cracked up. "That would be perfect."

"And who's that bald guy with the world on his back? Don't tell me it's Atlas."

"He's some mapmaker. And *that*"—Garth pointed up ahead—"is the monument to Arthur Ashe."

"He fought in the Civil War?" Mike asked.

"Very funny. There was this really huge stink about whether or not they should put him on Monument Avenue or tuck him away in some tennis court."

"Where he wasn't even allowed to play because of his *color* before he became famous," Lisa added.

"Well, the South in general isn't known for its progressive thinking," Mike said.

He turned a block past the Ashe monument and headed back toward the Fan District on Patterson. The houses were nice and well kept, for the most part. In one window, a Confederate flag hung as a curtain.

"See?" Garth said, pointing. "How crazy is that? And I still see bumper stickers that say things like 'Dern tootin' I'm a Rebel.' What's 'dern tootin,' anyway? It's not even English."

"It must be a special language called Southern,"

Mike said. "Very popular with the boondocks residents of Richmond, apparently."

"Richmond isn't the *boondocks,*" Lisa said. "It's a city."

"I guess by *boondock,* I meant 'backward.'"

"*Some* people are backward," Lisa clarified. "That's why it's so depressing to be smart and live here."

"Some people, of course." Mike shrugged. "But you made the point yourself: it's the South. I mean, I've been all over the country, and people from the South are a particular . . . breed."

"And what breed are *you?*"

Garth could detect a slight agitation in her voice. Her combative side was always ready to surface, in any situation. Maybe Mike had taken his South bashing too far—even though she was the one who'd started it.

"Midwestian," Mike said. "And I don't have a lot of good things to say about *that* breed, either."

They were turning onto Robinson Street now, on their way back to Lisa's house.

"Oh!" she said suddenly, leaning forward with her camera in her hand. "It's Mudpie! Can you slow down so I can get a shot of her, before she sees us?"

"Who's Mudpie?" Mike asked.

"An ex-drag queen who does nothing now but sit around on benches staring at people. Slow way down!

But don't stop. I want to get a candid shot."

Garth was uncertain as to how Mudpie had gotten her name (and was pretty sure he didn't want to know) and had never spoken to her, but she always seemed to be around. Or was she a he now? Drag queens, he knew from movies, liked being referred to by feminine pronouns. But did a drag queen who stopped doing drag go back to using the masculine pronoun? He had so much to learn. Mudpie was usually dressed in shorts and a dirty wifebeater, had an enormous belly, a filthy and apparently permanent plaster cast on one foot, and hair that sprang out from her head in arcing, twisted strands. Her face was set in a permanent scowl and she sneered at every passing car. He couldn't picture her back in her "show biz" days: on a stage, working to please an audience.

Mike slowed down and Garth bent into the dashboard so that he could fold his bucket seat forward. Lisa leaned into the opening and took one, two, three shots of the oblivious subject. Then Mudpie turned and caught sight of the Camaro—and the camera. A string of profanity spilled out of her mouth, most of it too raspy to be understood—and she raised her middle finger. Lisa took one last picture as Mike hit the gas.

"Fantastic!" she said. "Especially that last one."

"You can title that one 'Mayor of Freakville,'" Mike said, laughing.

Garth laughed, too, though Lisa fell silent in the backseat.

Mike dropped them both off back at Lisa's house. In her room, they put on the Kazooster CD and downloaded the pictures from her camera onto her laptop.

"I might shop in a little color," Lisa said, studying one of the images of Mudpie.

Garth flipped idly through a folder of printed photos. "Try brown. Wasn't Mike's reaction hilarious? He couldn't get over the fact that someone would go by the name Mudpie. He kept saying, 'Only in Richmond!' I think ol' Mud was his favorite part of the tour."

"I think he's a little full of himself, if you want the truth," Lisa said.

"Mudpie?"

"Your uncle," she clarified. "'Mike.' I think he's a little on the snobby side."

Garth hesitated. He knew Lisa could be judgmental; still, her comment surprised him. "What do you mean?"

"For one thing, he cast a pretty broad net with his comments on the South."

"You brought it up! And besides, you totally agree

with him. He didn't really say anything that you haven't already said to me—and to a lot of other people."

She clicked on the mouse, resizing the image. "The difference is, I'm *from* here. So I can trash it *and* know that a lot of people—including you and me—live here and aren't part of the . . . wave of dumbness, so to speak. He was just writing us *all* off as hicks."

"No, he wasn't!" Garth said. "He didn't mean it that way."

"'People from the South are a particular breed'? 'Mayor of Freakville'?"

"He was just trying to be funny. Listen—" He closed the folder and searched his brain for something that would make her like his uncle. "I *told* him. About me. Today. And he was fine with it. I mean, he was *totally* fine with it. So he's open-minded, I know."

"Maybe, maybe not. Don't get me wrong: I'm glad he doesn't have any problem with it. But I stick by what I said before. There's something a little too slick about him. Be careful."

"Be *careful*?" What did she think, that his uncle was going to knife them in their sleep? That he was going to rob them of house and home? (Not that there was much to rob.) Lisa, he decided, only had a sliver of the picture.

4

Peterson's Department Store ("Fine Products and Good Eatin' Since 1947!") sat on Broad Street and was probably half the size of a football field, but it felt a mile wide when Garth worked it. During any given four-hour shift, he had to sweep every aisle with a rickety push broom, mop the old terrazzo floor, and vacuum the rectangle of carpet that demarcated the women's clothing section. He had to restock the shelves, keep the stockroom organized, scrub down the men's and ladies' rooms—often while trying not to gag. Worst of all, he had to occasionally clean out what Mr. Peterson called the "trash pocket."

There were always surprises. The plethora of rats and mice that lived in the stockroom (when he'd walked through the double doors his first day on the job, he'd heard a scurrying beside him and had turned around in time to see a long, pink tail as thick as a finger curling out of sight behind a box). The pair of panties he'd found on the floor of the kitchen supply aisle (not a brand of panties the store carried). The graffiti in the bathrooms (more prominent in the ladies' room than in the men's, though less dirty). And the bizarre and truly disgusting list of items he'd had to dig out of the toilets by means of a coat hanger and rubber gloves: a plastic breath mint box, a set of keys, a Slinky (!), and, once, a cell phone that had startled the hell out of him by ringing as soon as he had it in his gloved hand (he hadn't answered it).

The graffiti in the men's room was, for the most part, stupid and occasionally insulting (as was Mr. Peterson's blanket order to "scrub those faggot words off the wall"). HERE I SIT ON THE POOPER, GIVING BIRTH TO A STATE TROOPER was one of the more recent additions, along with G.A.Y. = GOT AIDS YET? One long paragraph was written in tiny letters and described very specifically what the "author" wanted to do with another guy, and then named in graphic detail what he'd already done with guys in various public restrooms around town. IF YOU'RE INTERESTED, CALL ME, the paragraph concluded, followed by a phone number. Garth assumed that the person who could write such a thing would be gross, maybe even dangerous. He couldn't imagine having sex with a total stranger and certainly not in a restroom, but the thought that there were guys out there actually doing what he regularly fantasized about made him feel more isolated and hopelessly virginal than ever. People dropped dead every day, didn't they? Heart attacks, brain aneurysms, car crashes. What were the chances that he might die a virgin? Underneath CALL ME and the phone number, he'd written in pencil I WISH, and then hurriedly scrubbed all of it away.

He had nothing to compare his job at Peterson's to, since he'd never worked before, but it was hard to imagine more demeaning employment. Mr. Peterson, who'd been nursing a cold since the day he was born and yet still managed to talk through his nose, treated Garth like an idiot. He wouldn't even use his first name, would call him only "Rudd," stretching the one syllable out so that it might have emanated from a squeezed lamb.

"Rhhuudd, more bags on register two, pronto."

"Rhhuudd, mop up that *per*fume spill on aisle seven."

"Rhhuudd, there's a situation in the popcorn machine."

The "popcorn machine" was nothing more than a wheeled, plastic case with a heat lamp inside: a holder for the massive bags of stale, prepopped popcorn the store ordered in bulk. A "situation" usually meant a mouse.

Peterssuuun, Garth dreamed of saying one day,

*there's a pound of dandruff on your shoulders and you smell
like blue cheese and lighter fluid.*

The old man had to be close to seventy. Mr.
Peterson's dad had opened the store when he'd been a
teenager and then left it to him when he died. The store
was the only place Mr. Peterson, like Garth, had ever
worked. He was skinny and slope-shouldered, wore
black-framed glasses repaired (probably years ago)
with a safety pin at one of the temples, and suffered
back pain that prevented him from standing completely
upright. He moved about the store like a worn-out
prison guard, jangling his giant key ring and eyeballing each and every one of his employees with equal
mistrust.

That Tuesday, as soon as he saw Garth come in,
he called from across the stationery aisle, "Rhhuudd,
trash pocket."

Kill me, Garth thought. "I just did it two weeks
ago."

"And if you do a decent job this time, it might not
need it two weeks from now," the old man muttered.

I'd rather die a virgin than wade into that hellhole today,
he thought. But he knew he had no choice—not if he
wanted to keep his job.

The "trash pocket" was a sealed-off corner of the
stockroom accessible by a regular door on the inside

and a metal garage door on the outside. The garage door opened onto an alley where, in theory, and on some unspecified biweekly schedule that Garth could never keep track of, a garbage truck would appear, unlock and roll up the door, and empty the dozen or so trash cans into its bowels. The problem was that Mr. Peterson's employees—underpaid and overworked—didn't care about actually getting the trash *into* the trash cans; they simply opened the inner door and let the bags fly, including trash bags from the cafeteria that contained half-eaten food, spoiled food, rotten food. Add to that a few random holes punched into the walls over the years and a spigot near the floor in one corner that constantly dripped over a drain long-ago clogged, and you had a rodent's paradise. The bags were tossed from the doorway, missed their mark, burst open. The garbagemen refused to take the trash away unless someone gathered it into the cans. That someone, armed with a shovel and yet another pair of rubber gloves, was Garth.

As with the hedges on his chore list, he performed all of his other duties and saved the trash pocket for last. There was always the faint hope that some emergency might come up that would prevent him from getting to the pocket before his shift was over (say, a fire that would burn the store to the ground).

Unfortunately, that day, as slowly as he allowed himself to move without being obvious about it, he was still left with an hour on the clock; the old man made sure of it by telling him the bathrooms didn't require cleaning, and the vast floor needed to be swept but not mopped.

Groaning, Garth stormed into the back of the store, heard the regular chorus of scurrying claws (the creatures in the stockroom had long since stopped bothering him—at least they were on their way to somewhere else when he passed, which was more than could be said for the tenants of the pocket)—and gathered up the shovel and gloves. Having learned from experience, he tucked his T-shirt into his jeans and tucked the cuffs of his jeans into his socks. Then he opened the inner door.

The smell was horrific. And the little room, no more than five feet by seven feet, was alive: shifting, gnawing, and scraping with life—the pulse of ravenous diners. He reached a hand inside, felt along the wall, and switched on the single, bare lightbulb fixed to the ceiling. The only part of the floor not covered with trash was the corner where the spigot dripped. A pink-eyed, white-furred rat the size of an eight-week-old puppy crouched over the puddle, paused to sniff the air, then resumed drinking. In a nearby, torn-open bag of sour hamburger buns, a colony of gray mice climbed over one another, into and out of the tunnels they'd made. Something hidden under the refuse near the garage door bit or scratched something else; the something else squealed in anger—or pain.

Garth took a deep breath and set to work.

The task took nearly all of his remaining hour. The garbage was wet and the shredded plastic bags made the shoveling difficult. More difficult still were his efforts not to kill any of the mice or rats. (As much as they disgusted him, he didn't relish the idea of accidentally chopping one in half with the shovel blade.) The smaller ones crawled up his socks and latched onto his jeans until he swatted them away. The larger ones did their best to ignore him. Eventually, they all got the message, and those that weren't happily scooped into the trash cans with the rotting food moseyed back to the various holes in the walls and disappeared.

He had just finished scrubbing his hands in the stockroom's utility sink when he heard a scream from somewhere in the store. This was followed shortly by "Rhhuudd, aisle ten!"

He untucked his jeans from his socks and pushed through the double, swinging doors. An elderly woman was standing in aisle ten, her feet close together and her purse clutched under one arm. She was staring down, and when Garth rounded the corner, he saw Mr. Peterson crouching over the floor in front of her with a paper bag in one hand, a whisk broom in the other. "I don't know how this happened," he was saying. "It's the first one I've ever seen in this store, and I've worked here since I was a boy. It must have come in from outside."

"It's disgusting," the woman said.

"You're absolutely right. And I apologize."

He closed up the bag as she walked away. When he saw Garth, he frowned, handed him the bag, and said, "Take that into the stockroom and step on it, then throw it in the trash." Jangling his key ring, he started off after the woman hollering something about extra coupons.

Garth unrolled the top of the bag and looked into it. A small, gray mouse stared back up at him, its front feet testing the paper walls for traction and finding none.

He closed up the bag and carried it into the stockroom. When the swinging doors closed behind him, he squatted down, opened the bag, and poured the mouse out onto the cement floor. It stared at him for a moment without moving.

"Go make friends," he said, and watched it scurry away.

•   •   •

He came home that night to the smell of fresh paint. Mike had covered up the water stain on the living room ceiling with a coat of dull primer, which would be covered with ceiling paint once it was dry. He'd also repaired the screen door, replacing the screen and properly anchoring it into its track with rubber tubing. Both jobs were somewhat slapdash (the new screen had a slight sag in it, and Garth noticed a couple of paint drops on the living room carpet), but why hadn't it occurred to *him* to just do that?

Over dinner, his mom asked him how work had been.

"It was fine," he said. "Same old, same old."

"What do you do at this store?" Mike asked, turning his fork through his spaghetti.

"A little bit of everything. Cleaning, stocking, whatever needs done."

"But you like your boss," his mom said. "Mr. Peterson. You said he's nice to you."

"Yeah. He's great. A real joker, that guy." Garth forced a smile onto his face, and stuffed his mouth full of pasta.

"I have to say, I never had a boss I liked," Mike told them. "Not even the nice ones. It was just the idea of having somebody lord over me, telling me what to do, that didn't sit right with me."

"That's what most people call 'work,'" Garth's mom said.

"Mmmm." Mike sounded as if he were half humming, half growling. "You're channeling my brother, I think."

"It's true," she said. "Even bosses have bosses."

"Jerry didn't have a boss. He owned his own hardware store."

"Well, he had investors . . . " She trailed off. Garth wasn't sure if Mike knew the whole story. Not even Garth or his mom had known the truth until after his dad had died: the business had been struggling for some time and things had been much worse than his dad had ever let on. There was a bank loan his mom had no knowledge of. Personal loans from other businessmen. Of course, it had never entered his dad's mind that something might happen to him. The fallout of all that shaped their daily lives now nearly as much as their grief and healing—if, indeed, there was any healing going on. Sometimes Garth wondered.

"I guess there's always someone to answer to," Mike mused. He folded a piece of bread and dipped it into the sauce on his plate. When he was done chewing, he said, "So, not to change the subject, but Garth told me about his, uh, orientation."

Not to change the subject? It was all Garth could do to keep the pasta he was trying to swallow from funneling into his lungs as he saw his mom's eyes cut over to him. "Mike's family. You said it was all right to tell family," he explained.

There was a long pause while she thought about this. He knew she'd been put on the spot. Thankfully, she rose to the occasion. "You're right, I did say that. And Mike *is* family. I'm sure he understands how . . . delicate . . . this topic is."

"Oh, yeah, I totally get it," Mike said, nodding. "I was telling Garth how I've had gay friends before, and how they struggled with being in the closet and with coming out."

"We're not thinking about it in terms of his being 'in the closet.'"

True enough, Garth thought. In the very few words they'd exchanged on the subject, they'd never once used the word *closet.*

"Well, I'm just saying I've known people who've stifled who they were because they were afraid, and all of them, hands down, look back and wish they hadn't."

Who could argue with that? Garth felt his embarrassment at Mike's having blurted out the subject slipping away. Instead, he was beginning to feel grateful.

But his mom said, "Garth is only fifteen; he's not

necessarily ready to . . . defend himself . . . against people who might have certain prejudices, and we've agreed that waiting to explore this impulse is for the best."

"Impulse?" Garth said.

"Orientation."

"I really don't mean to stick my nose in where it's not welcome," Mike said, raising an open palm. "It's just that, you know, he's my nephew."

"Well, I'm his mother."

"And I totally respect that. But I was thinking that an outside voice—from someone in the family—might be helpful. I'm sure it took a lot of guts for Garth to tell you, and maybe there's room for him to—"

"Mike," she said, "I know you mean well, but don't overstep your bounds."

"No, no, no," Mike said, holding up both hands now. "I don't mean to do that at all."

"Lisa has gay friends," Garth suddenly blurted out.

His mom glared at him.

"She even broke up with a guy she was dating last year because he called her gay friends 'fags' and said they should all be put on an AIDS island," he said. "She told him to get lost."

"That kind of person is *exactly* why I worry about you telling people," she said. "What do you think that boy would have done if he'd known that, or even thought that, about you? He and his ignorant friends could decide to go after you, and how would you defend yourself?"

"Well," Mike said, sounding much calmer than Garth's mom; he almost sounded like the good-guy attorney on a TV drama, exploring all the angles of a situation, "he could defend himself with words. He could be ready to say, 'Hey, guys, just look at me as one less man in competition for all those girls out there.'"

"That sounds like the perfect way to get into a fight," she said. "Honestly, Mike, you don't know what you're talking about."

"Times have changed."

"They haven't changed that much."

"Well, Garth was telling me about this organization. What's it called? Rosemary?"

"ROSMY," Garth said.

"They apparently have all these services for teenagers *and* parents, and it sounds to me like—"

"You know what?" Garth's mom said, the volume of her voice raising slightly. "You're not a parent. You don't know what it's like to have an immediate family, lose half of it, and be worried about the safety of the other half. And I do. So . . . forgive me for putting my foot down, but I don't want to hear about ROSMY anymore. I'm Garth's mom, his only parent, and he's my responsibility until he's an adult."

Garth looked at Mike, who was still staring down at what was left of his spaghetti, his mouth not grinning now but pursed. Was he irritated? Pensive? Regretting that he'd brought up the subject in the first place? He put his elbows on the table and folded his hands together over his plate. "Actually," he said in a softer voice, "I *do* know what it's like to lose half my family. My dad passed away, so I've got my mom and my twin brother. Then my brother's suddenly gone. So I know what it's like. But you're right: I'm not a parent. I just want what's best for Garth here."

Garth was still feeling grateful, but he also had the vague sensation of being an object—like a piece of furniture in an empty room, with two people standing over it, deciding where it should reside. Yet he thought Mike understood him better than his mom did, or at least was willing to acknowledge that the decision about *where* the piece of furniture was placed wasn't so obvious, so . . . cut and dry. Neither Mike nor his mom was saying anything. He wanted to break the silence, so he said, "I want what's best for me, too."

His mom cleared her throat, pushed up from her

chair, and said, "There's ice cream, if anyone saved room for dessert."

His uncle stopped by his room that night, just as he was getting ready for bed. "Got a minute?" Mike asked.

"Sure." Garth was sitting on his unmade bed reading an old dog-training manual.

Mike looked at the title. "You going to teach Hutch some new tricks?"

"Nah. I just like reading this stuff. Did you know you shouldn't give your dog a one-syllable name because it'll take him longer to learn it?"

"Good thing neither one of us is a dog, then." Mike was in cargo shorts and a Grateful Dead T-shirt. He had a little bit of a gut, Garth noticed for the first time. He wasn't holding it in, either. He seemed comfortable with himself.

Garth folded his legs up and Mike sat down at the end of the bed. His brow was furrowed and his hands were working around an imaginary object, as if he were shaping clay on a spinning wheel. "I don't want you to think your mom and I are at odds," he finally said. "That's the last thing you need—your uncle coming into town and fighting with your mom."

"I don't think that," Garth said, even though that was exactly what he'd perceived at dinner.

"The thing is, when it comes to the whole gay thing, I know you don't agree with your mom." He looked Garth directly in the eye until Garth nodded. "And neither do I. But I understand where she's coming from. She's exhausted. I mean, she's overworked, and she's worried about you, and she loves you; I get all that. I mean, that's real stuff. There's a burden on her. I can see it when I look at her and hear it when she talks. What she's been through . . . honestly, I can't imagine what it was like for her. Or for you. Right now, I just want to be there for you and her both, you know?"

"Yeah," Garth said. Was he agreeing to something? Committing to something? He wasn't sure; he was just glad Mike had stuck up for him and was glad this late-night visit wasn't to say anything bad about his mom. "She works really hard. And, like I said, she's been kind of overprotective since Dad died."

"She's been through hell," Mike said. "So have you. I just hope I can help *both* you guys out while I'm here."

Again, Garth had no idea what the right response might be.

"Seriously," Mike said, and tapped his index finger against his temple. "I've got the wheels spinning on how to help."

"Thanks," Garth said.

"There's a mall nearby, right?"

"Willow Lawn isn't too far away."

"Do you want to go with me tomorrow? I could really use some new clothes. My shirts are played out, and I have some other shopping I need to do."

Tomorrow was a Wednesday, his volunteer day at Bone Sweet Bone. But what was one more day at the dog shelter compared to a day with Mike, who wasn't going to be here for very long? The more time Garth spent around him, the more he liked him. He could call Lisa in the morning and explain. He could call the shelter's number and leave Ms. Kessler a message saying that he needed one of the other volunteers to replace him. No big deal.

"Sure," he said. "Let's go."

5

Mike recognized the part of town they were in. Garth was directing him toward the mall, and while Broad Street pretty much looked like Broad Street block after block, Monument Avenue, west of I-95, became very suburban: apartment complexes, ranch houses, two-story homes with wide lawns, chain-link-fence-lined yards, oaks and pine trees growing in abundance.

"We're near the cemetery, aren't we?" Mike asked, guiding the Camaro with one wrist resting casually on top of the steering wheel.

"Sort of. This is the way we took to get there—"

"—the day of the funeral. I remember this stretch of road. I got to the funeral home just in time to follow you guys out here."

They rode along in silence for a mile or so. The sky was bright and clear, the sun burning through the windshield despite the car's air-conditioning.

"Would you mind if we . . . ?"

"No, it's fine," Garth said. He'd been half expecting the request. "I can tell you how to get there."

They passed the turnoff for the mall and drove up Monument till they reached Three Chopt Road. Ten minutes and a few turns later, they were at the entrance.

Garth had been out here with his mom frequently, at first, and then once a month since she'd taken on the second job. It wasn't a fancy, old-fashioned cemetery. It was clean and meticulously laid out and overwhelmingly level—as if someone had steamrolled the land before digging the first grave. There were very few upright headstones; most were just flat marble markers with brass plates, barely visible from a distance. Mike slowed the Camaro to a crawl and followed Garth's directions for which lane to take.

"It's right here," he said, and they rolled to a stop.

"Hard to recognize the spot without the canopy and folding chairs," Mike remarked, peering through Garth's window.

They got out, and were immediately engulfed in heat. Garth knew the way by heart: five markers over, four in. Then they were standing in front of the marble square fixed with the brass plate that bore his dad's name. The brief thirty-five years his life had spanned. The engraved phrase that they couldn't afford but that his mom had insisted on adding: LOVING HUSBAND, DAD, AND FRIEND.

The two of them stood at the foot of the grave in silence for a little while. Then Mike said, in a soft, uncharacteristic voice, "Hi, Jer."

"He can't hear you," Garth said, embarrassed by his uncle's presumption that he could just "talk" to his dad so easily.

"I know whatever's in *there* can't hear me," Mike said. "But that doesn't mean he isn't"—he stirred the warm air with a finger, indicating the cemetery, the surrounding suburb, the whole world, for all Garth knew—"listening." He cleared his throat and said, "Anyway, Jer, I came through town for a visit, and Sonja and Garth have been nice enough to take me in. They're doing great, by the way. I think your boy's grown a couple of inches."

He's lying to the dead, Garth thought. For his sake or his dad's? He stepped around the grave to the marker, bent down, and began pulling at the weeds that had grown up around the base.

"I'm sorry we didn't always get along, Jer. I think about you a lot. If I'd had any idea something was going to happen to . . . erase . . . either one of us so suddenly, I would have, you know, made more of an effort to stay in touch. Keep on good terms. I don't know.

I guess you just can't predict anything. You take the most important things for granted without even knowing you're doing it."

Garth stood up and dusted his hands together. When he looked back at his uncle, he saw that his eyes had gone damp.

Mike dragged a thumb over each eye and said, "I'm sorry."

Should he take his hand? Hug him? Garth had never thought much about it before, but he wasn't very good with physical contact—or hadn't been for the past year and a half. When people touched him, he tended to flinch. When he felt moved to touch someone else—even his mom—he did so awkwardly. "You don't have to apologize," he said.

Mike sniffed. "I, ah, wasn't talking to you."

"Oh. Sorry."

His uncle smiled. "*You* don't have to apologize, either. None of this is easy . . ."

Garth nodded. "Mr. Holt is buried over there," he said, pointing to a marker several rows over.

"Who's Mr. Holt?"

"The other man. The one who—"

"Oh, right. Of course."

They walked over and paid their respects to the man who had died with Jerry Rudd. "We used to be pretty close to the Holts," Garth said. "I went to school with Sarah, and Mr. Holt and Dad were good friends."

"You don't see them anymore?"

"They moved to Atlanta not long after the accident."

Mike squatted down next to Mr. Holt's marker and dragged a hand over it, as if reading Braille. He raised his head, and peered around at the expansive sea of graves. "You guys went out too far," he said in a low voice. Was he talking to Mr. Holt now as well? "You took too much of a risk."

The accident slide-showed through Garth's mind all over again. "I have this nightmare," he said. "I see them in the storm. I see them struggling, and then— they go down."

"That's not good."

"It's awful. But I haven't had it once since you got here."

Mike nodded—but cautiously, as if unsure whether or not it was okay to take credit. "All right," he finally said, and stood up. "Enough with the heavy stuff. Want to move on?"

Garth did. He never minded going to the cemetery, but once there, he never wanted to linger. Going seemed to serve a purpose; lingering was just depressing.

They followed the narrow asphalt strip, circling the grounds as they made their way back to the front entrance. At the other end of the cemetery, a funeral was under way. It wasn't a large affair: maybe half a dozen cars behind the hearse, a single row of chairs, the familiar blue canopy.

"You never know where the day's going to take you," Mike said softly as they crept past.

At the mall, Mike bought himself a few dress shirts and a pair of pants. He tried on some shoes, decided against them, then eyed Garth's worn-out sneakers and said he could do with a new pair. Garth didn't want Mike spending any money on him, but Mike insisted and wouldn't even let him pick out anything that was on sale. Did he know his mom's shoe size? Garth had no idea, so Mike bought Sonja a gift card she could bring to the store and use whenever she wanted. Garth carried his old shoes out in the box and wore the new ones, which were white with blue laces and—he had to admit—looked pretty cool. He thanked Mike repeatedly, until Mike finally waved him off: "They're just shoes." Before leaving the mall, they ducked into a gift shop, and Mike bought an oversized, decorative photo album for Garth and his mom to fill with the photos he'd given them.

"Where's a good lunch place?" he asked as they were nearing home.

"Turn here."

They parked on Cary Street, and Garth led the way to the Galaxy Diner.

Just as he'd done at The Tobacco Company, Mike told Garth to "order large." Here, that meant a bacon double-cheese burger, curly fries, a few side orders, and a chocolate milk shake. Mike ordered the same.

"I don't think I've ever had a fried pickle before," he said when the food came. He bit into it.

"Like it?"

"Yeah, actually." Mike's chair faced the street, and he gazed out the window as he ate. People flowed in and trickled out. "Hoppin' place."

"You mean the diner?"

"Yeah—and the whole block. It's like another mall, but without a roof."

"It's called Carytown. It's sort of like its own little village."

"A village with some beautiful ladies," Mike said, his eye following a woman as she walked down the sidewalk past the diner. Garth glanced behind him. Two more women were coming from the opposite direction, walking together, both on cell phones. "Yeow," Mike said. "That one on the right looks like my ex. Reminds me of why I hooked up with her in the first place."

The comments sounded just as crude to Garth as when he heard jocks talking about girls at school. Then again, he'd probably be doing it too, if he could. Somehow, Mike picked up on this. "It must be a bummer not being able to *say* anything, when you see some guy you think is good-looking. Not even being able to make a casual remark."

"Yeah, it pretty much sucks," Garth said.

"Mind if I ask you a personal question?"

"No."

"Have you ever, you know, done anything?"

"Had sex? That would be a big fat *no*." He looked down at the table and fiddled with his straw wrapper, a little embarrassed. He'd taken sex ed in the seventh grade and had felt like he'd learned everything he *didn't* need to know—sort of like suffering through calculus when you never planned on using it. "Why?"

"Just curious. You're definitely at the age where your mind's got to be reeling all the time—"

Correct, Garth thought.

"—and your mom means well, but she's kind of got you in a straitjacket."

Correct again.

Mike chuckled. "No pun intended. I'm just a little worried you might go nuts in it, at some point. People start . . . exploring . . . pretty young."

"So I've heard," Garth said. In truth, he really hadn't heard much—but he was curious. "How old were you?"

Mike smiled. "Fifteen. Mary Dalton was her name. I thought I'd have to twist her arm, but she was the one who made the first move."

Garth stirred a curly fry through the mustard on his plate. "Things . . . worked out okay?"

"Let's just say sex means different things to different people. It can be great, *really* great, and it can be lousy. And it can feel like love when it isn't love at all; it's just . . . sex."

"I wouldn't know."

Mike studied him for a moment. "Let's take a walk," he said.

He paid the bill, and as he accepted his change, he asked the man behind the register—point-blank, calm as could be—if there was a gay bookstore in the neighborhood.

For as full as his stomach was, Garth felt it fold in on itself.

But the man didn't bat an eye. Yes, he told them, there was a gay bookstore not far away. He gave them directions. Mike thanked him, and they left.

"I can't believe you asked him that!" Garth said,

once they were out on the sidewalk.

"Relax," Mike told him. "The world isn't quite the battle zone your mom thinks it is."

They walked several blocks and took the side street the man had mentioned.

"*You're* going in?" Garth asked. He hadn't given it any thought till now, but he'd assumed Mike would just wait outside for him.

"If you're up for it."

"But aren't you worried people'll think *you're* gay if you're seen in there?"

"What do I care?"

"Are you human?" Garth asked.

Mike laughed. "Last time I checked."

"You're so not what I think of when I picture the average grown-up straight man."

"Well, I'll take that as a compliment, too. I just think people should be able to be who they are, and be with who they want to be with."

They'd reached the bookstore. A large rainbow flag hung on a pole sticking out from the front of the building. "Ready?" Mike asked.

"I guess so."

They went inside.

Garth, of course, already knew of the store's existence; Lisa had told him about it the day he'd come out to her and had offered to take him there, but he'd always been too nervous to do it. Somehow, with Mike, he wasn't quite so nervous. In fact, stepping into the store made him feel like one of those kids entering Willy Wonka's chocolate factory—which, he realized, made his uncle Willy Wonka (a hilarious thought). He pictured Mike bursting into song: *Come with me and you'll be in a world of pure imagination.*

But Mike had already wandered into the depths of the store and was surveying a rack of books. Feeling embarrassed, even guilty (*of what?*), Garth glanced at the woman behind the register.

"Hello," she said, and smiled.

"Hi."

"They've got some good stuff here," Mike said, waving him over. "Just keep your eyes off anything too racy."

There *was* a lot of "racy" stuff in the store. Photo books with half-naked men on the covers. Calendars. Comic books that basically looked like porn magazines with drawings instead of pictures. Garth wanted everything his eyes fell on.

"Here," Mike said. "Some of these books are geared for guys your age."

Garth read the back flaps, and they didn't sound fantastical or horrific or even dirty; they seemed to be about guys pretty much like him.

"Will you read them? I don't want to get them for you if you're not going to read them."

"Yeah," he said, nodding his head. "I'll read them."

"Good. Here, you should have some of these, too." Mike walked over to a table and gathered a couple of safe-sex pamphlets, a copy of the local gay newspaper, and—to Garth's shock—a handful of free condoms. "I'm not saying you have to use them. Well, yeah, you *have* to use them if you're going to . . . have sex. But the point is to have them. Hide them away in a drawer, if you want. Oh—and throw them out after a few months if you *don't* use them. They're like potatoes: eventually they go bad."

A few months? Garth thought. *A few years is more like it.* Still, he felt excited just to have them in his possession.

There were several racks of DVDs near the back of the store. He wandered over to them, and saw that one held porn and the others held regular movies with gay subject matter. He lingered in front of the porn rack until he felt Mike's hands on his shoulders, steering him away. "That's not why we're here, Mr. Minor." He repositioned Garth in front of the regular movies, then wandered off to another part of the store.

Nearby, a man was sifting through a stack of T-shirts. A woman old enough to be his grandmother flipped through a bin of calendars. And standing just a few feet away from him, he now noticed, was a guy around his age. He was tall and had sandy hair, and he was beyond good-looking ("an uberhottie," Lisa would have said).

Garth forced his gaze back to the movies. For lack of anything else to do, he selected one of the DVD boxes from the shelf and stared at it.

"Ugh," Mike said, stepping over and looking down at the box. "Can you pick one that isn't violent? That looks like something your mom would conjure up in her nightmares."

On the cover was a pair of guys in tank tops. One of them had a black eye and was holding his hands in the air. The other had a pistol leveled at the battered guy's face.

"Have you seen this one?"

The voice wasn't Mike's. Garth looked over and saw that the sandy-haired guy was holding out a copy of a DVD called *Beautiful Thing*.

"N-no," Garth said cautiously.

"It's not violent. At all. It's a great story—one of my favorites, in fact. I've probably seen it a dozen times."

"Hmm," Mike said. "May I?" He took the DVD case from the guy's hand and turned it over to read the back.

The guy offered Garth a slight smile. "You look familiar."

Perfect. First time ever in a gay bookstore, and he was spotted, tagged, exposed. He had no idea how to respond and was afraid his voice would tremble if he spoke.

Thankfully, the guy answered his own question. "I know, we had Ms. Davis's humanities class together last year."

"We did?"

"But they switched me into Mr. Alison's class after the first week—which is maybe why you don't remember me. Also, you're friends with Lisa Hogart, right?"

As soon as he heard Lisa's name, Garth realized that was where he'd seen him. In the cafeteria, at lunch, when Lisa held court every so often with her "fellow artists."

"I'm Adam," the guy said. He held out his hand. "Adam Walters."

Garth shook the hand, hoping his palm wasn't sweaty. "Garth Rudd."

There was a pregnant pause.

"And that old guy who's with me is my great-granddad," Mike said.

"Oh—sorry." Garth turned and said, "This is my uncle Mike."

"Hi," Adam said.

"How's it going?" Mike shook his hand, then said, "You a Richmonder?"

"Yeah. For the past couple of years, anyway. My family moved here from Seattle."

Mike glanced down again at the DVD. "So this looks good. You said it's one of your favorites?"

"Top five," Adam told them.

"That's a pretty solid endorsement. Look good to you?" he asked Garth.

"Sure," Garth said.

"I'll be right back." He walked away, leaving them alone in front of the movie rack.

"So . . . ," Garth said with a slight sense of panic, searching, ". . . Lisa."

"Yeah. She's a trip, isn't she?"

"You must be an artist—what does she call those things she holds in the cafeteria? Séances?"

"Ha. Salons. I've sat in on a couple, but I wouldn't say I'm an artist; I just want to make films. I haven't done much about it yet because I can't afford any decent equipment, but I'm studying it."

"Every time you watch a movie, I guess."

"Pretty much. Or TV. Or even just walking around. I see everything in terms of shots." He grinned, and Garth felt himself grinning back.

Aware of the fact that he didn't have anything to contribute to the conversation nearly as interesting as aspiring to be a filmmaker (*"I want to take care of sick animals?"*) he said, "So this is in your top five, huh?" Then he remembered that he wasn't holding the DVD anymore; Mike had it and everything else at the register, and was paying the woman behind the counter.

"There are actually a lot of great films here." Adam laughed. "A lot of bad ones, too. You have to wade through the garbage to get to the gems. So how do *you* know Lisa?"

"I've known her for a while. We met, like, three years ago? She's pretty much my best friend."

"She's intense."

"So we're all set," Mike said, approaching them, bag in hand. "I took your recommendation and bought the DVD."

"You won't be disappointed," Adam said. "I could watch it over and over again."

"Do you live in the neighborhood?"

"Just west of the Boulevard on Colonial."

Mike glanced at Garth. "That's close to us, right?" Then he looked back at Adam. "Why don't you come over sometime and watch the movie with us?"

Garth's mouth went dry. What the hell was Mike doing—playing matchmaker? He was beyond embarrassed, sure that Adam would hear the suggestion as some perverted invitation to an orgy. "He said he's already seen it a dozen times. He doesn't want to see it again."

"I'd love to," Adam said, laughing a little. "Maybe the thirteenth time will reveal a whole new subplot I've never noticed before."

"Great," Mike said.

There was a pause and they all just stood there, staring at one another.

"This is the part where one of you writes down his phone number and gives it to the other one, so that this might actually happen," Mike prompted.

"Right!" Adam fumbled through his pockets, then spotted a mug of rainbow-colored pens on a nearby shelf. On a scrap of paper from his wallet, he wrote out his phone number for Garth.

Garth took the paper from him. "Thanks," he said.

"Well." Adam took a step to the side. His head dipped in a goofy—and adorable—way, and he offered a little wave. "Nice meeting you both."

"Yeah," Garth managed.

"You, too," Mike said. "We look forward to movie night."

"Call . . . whenever."

Adam walked out of the store, glanced once through the front window, and then was gone down the sidewalk.

"What did you do *that* for?" Garth asked Mike. "He probably thinks we're perverts!"

"Actually, what you just witnessed is how people meet. Get to know each other. Become friends. They open their mouths, form speech, and make plans to see each other again. I'm telling you, it's been happening for *years*."

"Well, at the very *least* he thinks I'm after him."

"Would you chill out? I'll play chaperone, if you want, ease the tension. He's not going to think you're 'after him' if your boring old uncle's in the room. Anyway, consider today progress." He hefted the bag. "You've got new shoes on your feet, a bag of . . . gay goodies . . . maybe even a new friend. It's not panic time."

Mike was right. Garth didn't want to see it as panic time. He wanted to see it as the opposite, in fact. It was his mom who would do the panicking, if she found out.

"We can't tell Mom we were in here."

"Well, you didn't break your promise, exactly, but I agree: she doesn't need to know about it. She'd be all over my case if she found out."

True enough.

"So it's our secret, okay?"

Garth nodded. Just like when Mike had brought up Project Garth with his mom, he felt both thankful and uneasy.

"There's something else she can't find out about, too—something I've been working on that will have to be another secret."

"What's that?"

"Come on, I'll tell you about it on the way to the car."

Not that Garth had sensed anything *un*generous in his uncle's demeanor, but it came as a surprise to learn that Mike had done charity work in the past. After eavesdropping on the conversation with his mom about gambling and Mike's lack of interest in a real job, and hearing Mike talking on the cell phone to Marty and Stu about money they owed to someone named Phil, he'd assumed his uncle's line of work was more on the shady side of what *he* was used to—but nothing *too* shady, more the stuff of an old Hollywood movie. So where did charity fit into Mike's picture?

"Charity work," Mike told him as they were walking back through Carytown, "has saved my financial neck more than a few times over the past few years. I've done some work for an organization that's frontlining the fight against meninosis. Ever heard of it?"

Garth confessed he hadn't.

"That's part of the problem." Mike went on to explain that almost *no one* had heard of the disease, which was affecting thousands of children all over the country, and the organization he'd worked for was devoted to increasing public awareness and raising money for a cure. Some charities operated solely through volunteers; others had enough backing to pay people to work their drives.

"They *pay* you to do charity work?"

"Exactly. And I know what you're thinking. Why pay people when you can get volunteers?"

"Actually, I was thinking the whole thing sounds a little weird," Garth said.

"And why's that?"

"Well, if you're collecting money for some organization, and they don't know how much you take in, how do they know you're not stealing from them?"

"You're a sharp guy," Mike said. "Remember I told you that. But think of it this way: assuming you're *not* robbing the organization, the cut actually functions as an incentive. The harder you work a crowd, the more you pull in. The more you pull in, the bigger your slice. And the best thing about it—other than the money, which can be good if you know what you're doing—is that it's temporary work, and that beats the heck out of a *regular* job."

It still sounded a little strange to Garth. But then again, Mike seemed to know what he was talking about. In fact, he could have been reciting language from a training manual. And from what Garth knew about him, it made sense that Mike would go for temp work like this.

"So what does this have to do with us?"

"I'm thinking we should do it."

"Here?"

Mike nodded. "Just temporarily. To generate some bucks for your college fund."

Garth thought of how *some bucks* would be useful, in general. It might bring his mom a little peace of mind, for one thing. Still, he asked, "What do you need me for?"

"Hey, it's *your* college fund, not mine. Besides, when it comes to charity work, two people are always better than one."

Garth tried to picture them approaching strangers,

asking for donations. "Isn't it just like begging?"

"Completely different. It's charity. It's for a cause."

"So why couldn't Mom know we were doing it?"

Mike tsk-tsked out the side of his mouth and shook his head. "I just don't think she'd like the idea. She'd find *some* reason why you shouldn't do it—don't you think? I mean, how could she not, if she's such a worrier?"

Garth could easily imagine the frantic concern etching itself into her face. "Yeah."

"So we'll just keep it under wraps until we're done."

The idea of keeping such a secret from his mom didn't sit well with Garth. Then again, she was the one who'd made him promise to keep a *huge* secret from the entire world. And if Mike was right, this was something that could actually help them, whereas what she'd asked Garth to do was only making *him* miserable. "All right," he said.

"Really? Aces," Mike said. "I've still got some pamphlets in the trunk from the last time I did this. I'll call the organization tomorrow and make sure they're still current." They'd reached the Camaro.

"What about my job? And the shelter?" Garth asked, suddenly remembering he still had a life to tend to.

"What about them?"

"Well, they take up time. We'd have to work around them."

Mike thought about it. "I can't speak for the dogs, but as for the store—what's it called again?"

"Peterson's"

"You hate working there, don't you?"

"How could you tell?"

"Because it's written all over your face when you talk about it."

"I do," Garth confessed. "I *loathe* it."

"What's that, fifteen hours a week? At minimum wage?" Mike drummed his fingers on the top of the car and did some quick calculations in his head. "Quit."

"Quit my *job*?"

"The money we pull in will more than make up for your salary, I guarantee it. And I can front you whatever spending money you need."

"But don't I have to give, like, two weeks' notice?"

"That's a myth created by bosses."

"I don't know," Garth said. Just thinking about the idea made his stomach clench with nervous excitement. "Mr. Peterson wouldn't be too happy about that. He's pretty cranky."

"All the more reason. Don't be intimidated by him; just tell him you're out of there. And keep that a secret, too." Mike got in behind the wheel.

Garth felt himself grin as he pulled open the passenger door. The visit to the bookstore, Adam's phone number in his pocket, the prospect of being free of Peterson's, *and* bringing in some money . . .

Aces, as Mike would put it.

6

The next morning, both his mom and Mike were gone by the time he got up. A note slipped under his door read: "Out of your hair today. Need to take care of some business.—Mike."

He poured himself a bowl of cereal and ate it in front of the television. Then he dragged the building's trash cans from the curb to their spot in the backyard (yet another duty that shaved a little off the rent). Finally, he stole away to his room and, even though he knew he was alone in the apartment—save for Hutch, who was sprawled across the living room couch—he closed and locked the door so that he could look at his "bag of gay goodies."

The local gay newspaper Mike had picked up for him had a headline article about a lesbian couple fighting for custody of their son—the kid's natural dad wanted nothing to do with him, but the paternal grandmother was trying to snatch him out of his mom's arms (the court verdict was yet undecided). Another article was about a teenager in the Tidewater area who was suspended from school for wearing a T-shirt that read: GOD IS GAY. "Prove me wrong," David, a sixteen-year-old, was quoted as saying. "Tell me who I'm hurting and I'll apologize to them face-to-face. Otherwise, back off!" On another page were the results of a survey on sex combined with alcohol consumption, and opposite that, an advertisement for something called a "foam party" in Washington, D.C. The ad was flanked with shirtless men, some wearing baseball caps, all of them good-looking but most way too muscular for Garth's taste. Which made him wonder, did he even *have* a taste?

He examined the novels Mike had bought for him. Nothing about custody battles or circuit parties to be found there, though one of them was about a gay teen-ager caught up in the struggle to get himself and his younger sister away from an abusive, alcoholic dad. A little heavy for summer reading, Garth thought. The next novel was about a gay teen, his straight sister, and their competition for the same "new kid" at school. And the third was called *Tale of Two Summers*—what looked like a hilarious blog exchange between two best friends who were spending their first summer apart in different cities. That one he left at the top of the stack.

But where to *put* the stack? None of this stuff could sit out in the open, because if his mom saw any of it, she'd know they'd gone to the gay bookstore and that he wasn't exactly sticking to his promise. Looking for a hiding place made him angry all over again. Why couldn't his mom see things—*understand* things—the way Mike did? Why should he have to hide who he was? Adam Walters certainly wasn't hiding, and he didn't look any worse off for it. He looked happy, in fact. Resentfully, Garth shoved the newspaper and the books into the back of his closet (there was irony for you), then stood for a moment with the DVD in his hand, gazing down at the title.

Beautiful Thing.

One of Adam's favorite movies. Which was almost the only thing Garth knew about him. Well, that and his desire to make films. And his phone number. The slip of paper was still folded up and tucked into Garth's wallet, like a cookie fortune you wanted to keep so that it might have a chance to come true—though he wasn't sure if he would ever get up his nerve to call. Chances were Adam was just being polite and had given out his number only because Mike had been so forward. He probably had no intention of coming over.

Still, if Garth watched the movie now (which he very much wanted to do, having the house to himself), would that cancel out the chances that Adam might possibly, by some slim chance, accept the invitation if he *did* get up his nerve to call?

Superstition is for crazy people, he thought.

But he left the DVD unopened and stowed it behind his laundry basket, on top of the newspaper and books.

"So what's the word on your brother's drama?" Garth asked.

"Um, where were you yesterday?" Lisa replied.

He'd called Ms. Kessler and left her a message, but he suddenly realized he'd forgotten to call Lisa. "Oh—sorry. Mike asked me to go shopping with him."

"He couldn't go by himself? Did he need you to hold his hand?"

"Don't be mean. We were just hanging out, that's all. How was it at the shelter?"

"Great, if you weren't the only person there cleaning out twelve cages, dealing with a neurotic Doberman and a pit bull with a bladder problem."

"Wait, you were alone?"

"Hello? My partner—that would be you, the one who talked me into volunteering at the shelter in the first place?—bailed on me."

"I left a message with Ms. Kessler. I thought she'd

get someone to replace me."

"Didn't happen."

"I'm sorry," he said again. "So—what's the news on your brother?"

"Same as before. He wants to have the baby; his girlfriend wants to have the baby; my parents prefer to have a cow. How was the shopping?"

He could hear the irritation in her voice. While she could toss out insults right and left, she wasn't one to overlook even the smallest of slights. "To be honest," he said, "this really cool thing happened. Mike took me to that gay bookstore."

"The store *I* told you about?"

"Yeah."

"The store *I* offered to take you to, since you were too scared to go by yourself?"

"I don't think I ever said I was 'too scared.' Anyway, he took me and bought me all this cool stuff. And I met a friend of yours there."

"Who?"

"Adam Walters."

"Oh! Adam's great. A total sweetheart. *He'd* never leave me alone with a dozen dirty dogs."

"I said I was sorry!"

"I'm just giving you a hard time. Seriously, though, Adam's cool. He has 'honesty issues,' but he's a good guy. And gorgeous."

"What are 'honesty issues'?"

"He tried to date a guy last year who turned out to be a pathological liar. Now he says he doesn't know if he can ever trust anyone again, romantically."

"What did the guy lie about?"

Lisa laughed. "Being single, for one thing. Anyway, I could totally see you two as a couple."

"Right. He's about a foot taller than me."

"Who cares? Tell me you don't think he's hot."

"He is. But that's not the point. I'm just saying, I met him at the store and we talked. He told me about how he wants to make movies."

"Yeah, I call him Orson Smells."

"Very mature."

"Hey, he calls *me* Diane Arbutt."

"*Any*way, he gave me his phone number."

"Seriously? Are you going to call him?"

"I don't know. What would I say?"

"How about 'Hi, uberhottie that I just met. Want to have lunch?'"

"Shut up."

"Not my specialty. I *am* happy for you. I just wish you had let me be the one who ushered you into gay-dom, since I offered first."

"It sort of happened on impulse."

"Uh-huh. And how does this affect the pact you made with your mom?"

"I don't know. I didn't tell her."

"But Mike knows?"

"About the pact? Yes, he knows. He thinks it's crazy."

"Well, so do I. But I also think it's a little weird that he'd take you there knowing it's not what your mom wanted."

"As you just pointed out, *you* offered to take me there."

She clucked her tongue. "Yeah, but I'm an irresponsible teen."

She's jealous, he thought. *And she's mad that I didn't show up at the shelter.* He decided to drop the subject— and to not mention the charity work (she'd have plenty to say about *that*, for sure). It was funny how the people with the toughest exteriors were sometimes the ones whose feelings got hurt so easily.

As promised, Mike "fronted" Garth some spending money—fifty dollars, which was nearly a month's worth of what he allowed himself—and on Saturday, per his uncle's suggestion, Garth worked his last shift at Peterson's Department Store. He commemorated the event by unlocking and rolling up the garage door

114 •

of the trash pocket in order to liberate as many mice and rats as possible, but they didn't seem very interested in leaving (which made sense when he thought about it—why give up the safety and convenience of all that rotten food for the big, unknown world?).

"Rhhuudd," Mr. Peterson said as he was about to clock out. "Truck's coming in next Saturday. I need you to work."

"I've already made plans."

"Got to cancel them. It's a big shipment."

"Um." Garth punched his card, put it back into its metal slot, and stared up at the old man. He knew what he was about to do was abrupt, but he also heard the echo in his head of Mr. Peterson's voice saying, "Scrub those faggot words off the bathroom wall." And once, while complaining about a customer who'd returned a humidifier, the word *uppity* had rolled out of his mouth, followed by the *N* word. "I quit," Garth said.

Mr. Peterson's lined face went slack with what seemed to be confusion, then slowly pruned into a scowl. "You ever had a job before this one?"

"No."

"If you don't give two weeks' notice, I don't have to issue a check for this pay period. How's that sound?"

Garth was fairly certain that wasn't true—or legal. "I'll make you a deal," he said, surprised at his own boldness. "I quit today, you pay me for the hours I've worked, and I won't call the Health Department about the mouseketeer club in the storeroom, the kitchen, *and* the popcorn machine. How does *that* sound?"

Peterson gauged him for a moment, and his scowl leveled off into a smile that was a half sneer at best. He reached forward to shake Garth's hand, but with his other hand he took hold of Garth's elbow and squeezed sharply. He knew what he was doing; the pain shot from Garth's arm into his chest and even down his legs. "Guess we've got each other figured out," the man said, still squeezing his elbow. "You're not Peterson material."

"Lucky me," Garth said, wrenching his arm free.

"You can pick up your check next week."

"Thanks," Garth said. For better or for worse— even if the charity work was a flop—he was forever free of The Trash Pocket.

Sunday afternoon, Garth rode his bicycle downtown and chained it up next to the footbridge that led out to Belle Isle. Dressed in his bathing suit, T-shirt, and flip-flops, he walked across the bridge listening to the thunder of traffic overhead—a sound that was gradually replaced by the rush of the James

River as he neared the opposite shore. All along this stretch of the island were rocks—light brown and worn smooth over centuries, perfect for lying out in the sun. And there was a *lot* of sun—too much of it, in fact; by the time he reached Lisa, he was drenched in sweat.

She had her eyes closed and was stretched out on her back on a bright blue towel. She'd brought her camera, of course, and her cell phone, and her iPod—all laid out alongside her in case she needed them. He set his towel down next to hers, kicked off his flip-flops, and quietly picked up her camera.

When she heard the click, she lifted her head and glared at him. "Did you just take my picture?"

"I did," he said. "You look like a model."

"As if you'd know."

"Hey! I can still tell whether or not a girl's hot, even if I don't go for them."

"Don't ever do that again. Photographers should only take their *own* portraits. The ones who are artists, anyway."

He sat down on his towel and pulled his shirt over his head. "That sounds like a rule you made up for yourself."

"Artists *need* to make up their own rules. They can't follow the existing rules because it would make them—"

"Yeah, yeah. Soulless. I've heard it before. Could it be any muggier out here?"

"A few more years of global warming, it'll be muggier."

"I'm going to dunk myself to cool off."

"Okay," she said. "But hurry up, because I have big news to tell you." She rolled over onto her stomach and closed her eyes again.

He worked his way from one rock to the next, farther and farther out (impossible to do when the water level was higher), and when he ran out of rocks, he sat down, held on with his hands, and sank his legs in. The water was chilly, despite the heat, and he felt the current tugging gently at his feet. He stayed like that for several minutes before easing down into water up to his shoulders; then he pulled himself out and stood dripping on the sunbaked surface of the rock. It was the closest he'd ever got to swimming since his dad had died. Not that he was afraid of drowning, but the idea of enjoying himself in or on the water just felt wrong somehow. A pair of kayakers threaded past, bound for the rapids that started farther south. One of them waved at him; he raised a hand in response.

Hello.

Be careful.

Where the hell are your life vests?

"So," Lisa said when he got back, "my news."

"You have a new boyfriend."

"Who told you?"

"No one. A new boyfriend is *always* your news. Besides, it's been, what, two weeks since you've dated anyone? That's quite a dry spell for you."

"You make me sound like a slut."

He grinned. "A virgin slut."

"*Any*way, don't you want to know who it is?"

"Who?"

"The one and only—" She paused for dramatic effect. "Billy Fillmore."

Garth drew a blank for a moment. Then he said, "The quarterback?"

"Halfback." She extended her neck and smiled proudly.

"You're dating a *jock*?"

"Tell me you aren't jealous."

He thought about it. "I'm not."

"Oh, come on! He's gorgeous!"

"Not my type." Garth shrugged.

"Having never dated anyone, you don't get to have a type."

"That was harsh."

"It was, wasn't it? Sorry. I try to spare you my mean

side. I'll be making it up to you in a few minutes, in any event."

"What do you mean?"

"Never mind, it's a surprise," she said, smoothing out her towel. "I can't believe you don't think Billy Fillmore is droolworthy. Wait till you get to know him."

"I'm not sure I want to."

"Why?"

"Well, have you ever seen those movies about Vietnam, where the soldiers don't want to get to know any of the new recruits because they probably aren't going to survive for very long?"

"Wow. Now who's being harsh?"

He grinned and said, "Me, for a change."

"Oh! Here comes your surprise." Her eyes darted toward the path that led from the footbridge.

Garth looked over and saw Adam Walters approaching them.

Adam had a towel in one hand, his shirt in the other. He wore only bright red bathing trunks and a pair of sneakers.

Garth turned back and glared at Lisa.

"Your uncle isn't the only one who can help you come out," she told him.

"Hi," Adam called as he drew near. "You guys were

easy enough to find." His dense sandy hair flashed in the sun.

"My favorite spot on the island," Lisa said, stretching out. "I think you've already met Garth."

"Yeah. We go all the way back to . . . Wednesday." Adam smiled and reach a hand down toward Garth.

Garth got to his feet—and immediately regretted it because of how much taller Adam was than him. He was self-conscious, too, about his hair (unwashed and unruly), about his legs (ultraskinny, like pipe cleaners), and about his stomach (which was flat enough but soft, and absent of the ridges he could see in Adam's). "Hi," he said, shaking the hand. "I—I didn't know you were coming."

"Me either. Till about an hour ago."

"The magic of cell phones," Lisa said.

Adam glanced at the wet footprints still visible on the rock. "Looks like one of you has already been in the water."

"Just to cool off," Garth said. "The water's actually pretty cold."

"I guess I'll bake myself for a little while first." He spread his towel out on the rock next to Garth's and lay down on his back. After a few moments, he rolled over with his head turned away. "I had to wash both my parents' cars this morning," he muttered. "Guess it was the head start on my tan."

Garth let his eyes linger undetected on Adam's smooth back, the nape of his neck, the slope of his shoulders. Correction: *not* undetected. Lisa was observing this examination. He caught her gaze and bugged his eyes out at her. He really didn't know whether to scowl at her for putting him in this spot, or thank her.

"It's a wonderful view, isn't it?" she said, then immediately added, "The skyline, I mean. All that green, and then all that silver." She nodded toward the buildings downtown, across the river.

"Yeah," Garth uttered. "It's great."

"I can't decide whether it's more impressive from a distance, or when you're right up close to it." She arched an eyebrow, then lay down herself.

He remained propped up on his elbows. Next to Adam, he felt like a squishy little (he hated thinking the word almost more than he did hearing it come from someone else's lips) shrimp. Was this what being attracted to someone else of the same sex—in such close proximity (and with so much exposed flesh)—had to be like? Did you have to see your own bodily faults in order to appreciate their assets?

Relax, Mike would have told him if he were here. So he decided to.

He lay flat, closed his eyes, and listened to the treetops

stirring in the slight breeze. The traffic clopping over the bridge. Farther down, the rapids—so faint that he might have been imagining the sound. When he opened his eyes again and glanced over, Adam had his head bent back and was squinting at the woods that stretched out behind them.

"There used to be a prison on this island, right?"

"The whole *thing* used to be a prison," Garth said.

"It would make a good white-collar prison," Lisa put in. "With a spa and mud baths—and nature hikes."

"Well, it wasn't *that* kind of prison," Garth said. "When the North took the city, they just stuck all the Confederate soldiers out here with no food, no supplies, nothing. They had to, I don't know, eat each other to survive."

"That's disgusting," Lisa said. "And you know what? When we read about that in American History, I thought, The river's not that wide. Why not just swim back to civilization?"

"Because there were guards posted all along the bank. They'd shoot you if you tried."

"Oh," she said. "Ouch."

"Yeah, ouch," Adam echoed. "But I was just thinking, that would be a great story for a film. A love story, in fact."

"A *love* story?" Lisa asked.

"Yeah. Two prisoners stuck out here on this island, fighting to survive. One helps out the other in some skirmish, and they bond, fall in love."

"Sort of like *Romeo and Juliet* meets *Escape from New York*?" Garth asked.

Adam laughed. "Exactly! Well, *Romeo and Romeo* meets *Escape from Belle Isle*."

"The problem with that idea," Lisa said, "is that it would have to be about a bunch of Confederate soldiers. That would be like making a love story starring Nazis. It can't work. No one would sympathize."

"I disagree," Adam said. "You're taking brain-washed kids off farms and putting guns in their hands, sticking them on the front lines, giving them no choice. You can't expect them all to rise to your moral standards."

"Plus," Garth said, "you could always have your characters become a little . . . conflicted about the cause."

"Right? That's what would make the story interesting! Conflict and the steamy island sex."

"Wait," Lisa countered. "Two rebel soldiers having sex? That's hot?"

Adam glanced at Garth. "Hello?"

"That is so twisted," she said.

Garth shrugged.

"I have a project in mind, too," Lisa said. "I want to photograph my probably soon-to-be sister-in-law once a week throughout her pregnancy, naked—her, not me—and then once a week naked with my niece-slash-nephew for the first ten years of her-slash-his life. Same pose, every time. I want to call it *129 Months*."

"That sounds like a recipe for one messed-up niece-slash-nephew," Garth said.

"Seriously," Adam grinned.

"Not everything is about sex," she declared.

"Oh? No one told me." He turned to Garth. "So what about you? Any artistic flair?"

"Flair?" Garth asked.

"Interest. Pursuit."

The wording threw him. He opened his mouth, then closed it. *You, at the moment,* he imagined saying.

"Garth," Lisa announced, "is going to become the world's greatest veterinarian."

"Really?" Adam asked him. "So you must have a lot of pets."

"No," Garth said, "just one dog—a springer spaniel named Hutch. We used to have a golden retriever named Starsky, too. My dad named them both; he was crazy about that show when he was growing up."

"Starsky and Hutch. Hilarious. What happened to Starsky?"

"My parents got him before I was even born. He lived to be twelve and a half. Then he kicked."

"Kicked! You don't sound like a very sensitive vet!"

"What do you want me to say? He passed on. Expired. Went to biscuit heaven," Garth said. "I don't have the compassionate vet lingo down yet, I guess."

"Don't listen to him," Lisa said. "Garth's going to be the Surgeon General of dogs."

Garth felt his face flush. He shrugged, deflected. "Who knows, I might not be a vet at all. I just want to work with animals in some way."

"You could join a circus," Adam offered. "Be an elephant trainer."

"Or the guy who cleans up the elephant poop," Lisa said.

"Thanks," Garth said. "You flatter me."

Adam turned toward him. "Did you watch the film, by the way?"

"Not yet." Garth was suddenly embarrassed, realizing that *Did you watch the film?* was just another way of asking, *Are you going to invite me over or not?* Fortunately, Lisa didn't know about Mike's suggestion, or she would have run with that one big-time, right there on the spot.

They drifted into silence. When Garth looked over

again, he saw that both Adam and Lisa had closed their eyes and were basking in the sun. He felt as if he'd missed some signal that it was nap time (what was this, grade school?) and he closed his own eyes, wondering if he'd said something stupid to shut the conversation down.

What seemed like less than a minute later, he heard a rustling next to him. He glanced over and saw Lisa standing with her towel thrown over her arm.

"Where are you going?"

"Home," she said. "I have to get ready for my date tonight."

"With Billy Fillmore."

"The one and only."

"The quarterback?" Adam asked, pushing up onto his elbows.

"*Half*back," Lisa corrected, then went on to qualify: "That's twice a quarter. I'll see you boys later."

She apparently recognized the slight panic Garth knew was in his face, because she gave him a wry look and—blatantly, so that Adam could see—a thumbs-up.

When she was gone, Garth and Adam just lay there, both propped on their elbows, watching the river. Another kayak drifted by. Then a trio of middle-aged hippies on their backs in inner tubes, holding cans of beer. Adam scissored his feet back and forth. A jet passed high overhead, its engines briefly overlapping the sound of the river. They said nothing but just watched the river for what felt to Garth like a long stretch of time but was probably only a few minutes.

"Do you want to swim?" Adam asked, rising up into a sitting position.

"I was already in once."

"I know, but it looks like you've sufficiently dried out." He glanced at Garth's hair, his chest, even the fabric of his swimsuit. "Want to cool off again?"

Garth suddenly felt aroused, nervous, and frozen all at once. "You go ahead," he said. "I'll hang out here."

Adam stood, straightened the waistband of his swimsuit, and walked to the edge of the rock. His body—still pretty pale but a little pink now along the shoulders and around the back of his neck—was gorgeous. Sexy. *Hot.* Should he have offered to join him? Did his nervousness show, now that Lisa was gone?

Did Adam even care?

With the downtown skyline nearly hidden by the trees on the opposite bank, they might have been in a different world. Just as being around Mike was starting to feel like a different world from the one he shared with Lisa, or his mom. Or maybe he had that wrong. Maybe *he* was the one who was different around each of them. If that was the case, who was he now?

Yet another Garth in the act of figuring out the world.

He sat up as Adam slid off the farthest rock and down into the water. Garth kept him in his sight line, held him that way, as a narrow band of cloud snaked a shadow between them.

The next morning, after they'd finished breakfast and his mom had left for work, Garth caught Mike up on what was going on.

"And?" Mike said, pouring two mugs of coffee—one for him and one for Garth.

"And what?"

"What happened next? You don't have to give me the gritty details, but did you at least get some sort of signal from him?"

Signals? Garth wondered. Like referee hand gestures? Two tugs on the ear, one tap on the nose: *I think you're cool?* "We hung out for a while. He swam, I didn't. We talked some more, then rode our bikes back to the neighborhood and went our separate ways."

"So you got no sense at all that he's interested in you? As maybe more than a friend?"

Garth shrugged. "How would I even know?"

Mike groaned—as if he really had something invested in this and Garth was tampering with the market. He sipped his coffee, studied Garth for a moment, then said, "Let's talk about tomorrow."

"Okay."

"I called my contact at the charity organization and we're all set to go."

Contact? It sounded more like spy work than charity. "What does that mean?"

"It means we can use the old pamphlets. Unfortunately, there've been no new developments on the meninosis front since the last printing. I also bought us a card table, which is more effective as a 'base' for a charity drive than just walking up to people on the sidewalk. Oh—and poles for the banner."

"What banner?"

"There's always a banner. You think people are just going to walk up to a table on their own? Something has to catch their eye."

The more concretely Mike talked about the charity work, the harder it was for Garth to actually picture them doing it.

"So let's talk strategy," Mike said. "How are your acting skills?"

"My *what*?"

"You know—tragedy, comedy, the gamut in between. Can you act sad, if you have to? Not burst-into-tears sad, but gloomy. Woeful."

Garth was pretty sure he had gloomy and woeful down pat. But were they going to put on a charity *play*? A benefit performance? "I don't get it."

"There's nothing to get. We just need you to look convincingly sad about the cause and, most important of all, earnest."

"I *am* earnest," Garth said. "Aren't I?"

"No teenage angst. No *ennui*."

"What's 'on-wee'?"

"Never mind. Act like someone just slapped you, okay? Trust me, it'll help both the cause and us."

"What if someone I know sees me doing this 'act'?"

"I've thought about that. Which is why we won't be doing it in Richmond."

"We're traveling?"

"Just to nearby towns. You don't have to drive too far to be in some place like Hopewell or Mechanics-ville. So we're good to go?"

Garth had the sudden impulse to back out. It just wasn't in him, standing in front of strangers asking for money. Plus, the whole idea just didn't feel quite . . . right.

At the same time, he didn't want to disappoint his uncle. He also didn't want to come across as being too scared or "saintly" to do something a little edgy.

"I'll give it a try," he said reluctantly.

Mike lifted his mug as if toasting him. "That's the spirit." He finished his coffee and set the mug down loudly on the table between them. "Now that business is taken care of . . . are you going to call Adam?"

"What does he have to do with any of this?"

"Absolutely nothing. But are you going to call him?"

"That's still sort of up in the air."

"And it could stay that way forever. You've spent some time with him now. You ought to call him and invite him over so we can watch that *Beautiful* whatever it's called."

"*Beautiful Thing*," Garth said, thinking, *Since when did I become everyone's pet project?* He'd gone from feeling shoved into gay hiding by his mom to feeling yanked out of it twice over by Lisa and Mike. Couldn't there be a happy medium? Or couldn't these decisions be made by the person they most affected—namely, him?

Not an unreasonable thing to want, he decided, and took a long sip of coffee.

But who was he kidding? He was thankful to Lisa for inviting him to the river, and thankful to Mike for encouraging him to make the call. And if he was going to be doing something as weird as going along with Mike's plan in order to contribute to his college fund (as well as a charity), he might as well do something potentially good for himself on a personal level.

So long as his mom didn't find out about Adam. Or the charity work.

Or the trip to the bookstore.

Or the fact that he'd quit his job without telling her.

When did that list get so long?

7

"*MENINOSIS KILLS!*" The words dominated the front page of the pamphlet in thick, dark letters, the exclamation point a dagger over what looked like a lump of coal. Beneath the headline was the sentence, "Anyone, Anywhere, Anytime—But Most of All . . . CHILDREN." And below that, a photo of a child's face taken from such a close proximity that it was impossible to tell whether it was a boy or a girl, only that it was very, very sad.

Garth opened the trifold pamphlet and began reading. It only seemed appropriate that he be familiar with the disease if he was going to spend the day asking people to donate money for a cure. Meninosis, he learned, was related to scoliosis, spinal meningitis, and peritonitis. It affected the bones and certain vital organs, including the liver. It was believed for many years to be environmentally contracted—specifically, through the inhalation of fertilizer residue found on produce grown and sold throughout the U.S. Many years later, a second "contractual vessel" was discovered: plastic monourethane. This was a most frightening discovery, because by 1994 plastic monourethane—a petroleum by-product long since banned by the EPA—had already been used as insulation in many American homes.

"You don't have to read all that," Mike said. He was wearing one of the dress shirts and the pair of trousers he'd bought at the mall—much more formal than his usual T-shirt and jeans. He steered them along the entry ramp that funneled onto I-95.

"Don't you think I should know about it? If I'm going to be talking to people?"

"It's depressing. And anyway, you don't have to talk too much. That's what the pamphlets are for. All you need to say is, 'Please help us fight meninosis.' 'Meninosis kills.' 'Your dollars will help us find a cure.' Stuff like that." He was staring forward, watching the road and mirrors. "If anybody asks you a question, direct them to me."

Garth turned the pamphlet over and saw grotesque close-ups of twisted spinal columns, braised skin, a foot so deformed it looked like a shaved lion's paw. "Eww."

"Told you it was depressing."

"Have you ever known anyone who had it?"

The Camaro swept into the left lane, passed a pick-up truck, swept right again. "Thankfully, no."

"But you've seen people with it?"

"Sure."

Garth winced. "Deformed?"

"I can't really talk about it," Mike said, still staring at the road. "Let's just say, seeing it with my own eyes is what brought me to the cause."

He turned on the radio.

When they reached Hopewell—a town just thirty miles outside of Richmond—it was 10 a.m. They roamed around for a little while, checking out the businesses. Mike ultimately decided on a grocery store, doubled back to it, and pulled into the parking lot. He circled the lot, gliding right past the front of the store, and pulled into a space close to the street. "Can you manage that?" he asked, indicating the box of pamphlets.

"Yeah."

"All right. I'll get everything else."

Garth carried the box across the parking lot to the storefront. Mike carried two short plastic poles with round bases, a rolled-up banner, and a card table. They set up camp around twenty feet away from the sliding entry doors. "You mainly want to get them when they're going in, not coming out," Mike said under his breath as he doubled and then tripled the length of the telescoping poles. "When they've got free hands and money in their pockets. And when they *haven't* just coughed up a hundred dollars for a week's worth of groceries."

"Shouldn't we be closer to the entrance?" Garth asked.

"Nuh-uh." He unrolled the banner (PLEASE HELP FIGHT MENINOSIS—YOUR GENEROSITY WILL SAVE LIVES!) and strung it between the poles. Then he set up the card table in front of it. "Hold tight. I've got to run back to the car."

As he left, a woman and her daughter were approaching the entrance. The daughter—around ten—read the banner, but the mom didn't even seem to notice it *or* Garth. They disappeared into the store.

When Mike returned, he had a plastic bag hanging from his wrist and was carrying a folding chair, a fishbowl, and a large blue plate Garth recognized from their kitchen. He set everything down, unfolded the chair, and placed it beside the table. From the bag he took a large package of Tootsie Pops, which he ripped open and poured onto the plate. Then he reached into his pocket and produced a small wad of bills (mostly singles, but a few fives and tens, as well) and dropped them into the fishbowl. Finally, he spread a handful of pamphlets across the surface of the table like cards fanned out for a magician's trick.

Garth gazed at the display, admiring how professional it looked. A moment later, he nearly jumped, startled as Mike's voice boomed across the parking lot.

"*Please* help us fight this horrible disease!"

He was standing beside the table, standing more erect than usual with a pamphlet held out before him. There were people approaching: women, mostly, some of them alone and some with children in tow.

"It's a *very* serious disease, with *very* serious consequences, affecting children just like yours and mine, friends!" Mike hollered. It was a particular way of hollering: loud, but not angry; emotional, but not accusatory. Garth thought he sounded like a preacher or a TV evangelist.

"Ma'am," Mike said in a voice toned down a few notches, "just a minute of your time?"

"No, thank you," the woman said, and carried on into the store.

"Miss?" Mike asked, extending the pamphlet toward another woman. "We're not asking for more than you'd pay for a can of soda. Meninosis is a terrible disease—but it doesn't have to be."

She slowed down, eyeing the banner.

"Even as children suffer, there's work going on for

a cure. Every day—and every dollar—brings us closer to it."

She accepted the pamphlet, but instead of reading it, she opened her purse and took several dollars from her wallet. As she dropped them into the fishbowl, Mike thanked her and god-blessed her, and she smiled and thanked *him*.

A man behind her was already digging into his pocket. His coins disappeared among the bills.

Mike glanced over his shoulder at Garth. "You want to help out a little, here?"

Garth looked at the money in the fishbowl. He looked at a couple crossing the parking lot, having just gotten out of their minivan. At a woman holding a baby and slowing down as she passed the table. At Mike, whose head was cocked in his direction expectantly.

"Meninosis kills!" he heard himself shout.

"*Easy,*" Mike instructed out of the side of his mouth.

"Meninosis is a serious disease!" he hollered at a somewhat lower volume.

"Better," Mike muttered.

"We need your generous support to fight the good fight!" Where had *that* come from?

But Mike was nodding his head, even as he held

out another pamphlet toward an approaching shopper. "And don't forget the emotion."

For a moment, Garth didn't know what he meant. Then it dawned on him. He took a deep breath, exhaled, and let his face deflate into what he hoped was a mask of sadness. "Please, folks! We *can* cure meninosis, but we need your help!"

"Hello, miss," Mike said, and then stood patiently as the woman examined the pamphlet he'd handed her.

"This is terrible," she said.

"It is," Mike confirmed.

"I've never even heard of this disease."

"That's part of the problem: public awareness. Even if people can't contribute financially today, at least they'll be made aware. That's the first step."

"It's terrible," the woman said again.

Garth's eyes widened as he watched her push a ten-dollar bill into the fishbowl. Mike thanked the woman profusely.

And so it went. At least half the people heading into the store ignored them, but the other half stopped to investigate and eventually contributed or simply dropped a dollar or two into the bowl as they passed without engaging either one of them. Some of the ones who'd ignored them going in, Garth noticed, had apparently reconsidered while they were shopping (or maybe they'd just needed to get change), because when they emerged they pushed their carts deliberately up to the table, money already clutched in their hands and bound for the fishbowl. The Tootsie Pops turned out to be a stroke of genius (Mike, no doubt, already knew this), because even if the parent had no intention of acknowledging the pamphlets and the banner and the charity workers, the *child* took notice of the plate of lollipops, and went for it. And once the lollipop was in the child's hand, the wrapper already torn halfway off, the parent seemed successfully guilted into contributing *some*thing to the cause. It was almost as if they were doing nothing more than selling lollipops, only nobody would pay five dollars for a lollipop, and some of the parents—once Mike had gotten hold of them and said a few words—did just that.

One very old man dressed in a suit and a bolo tie, his ancient wife on his arm, shuffled to a stop before the table and examined the display. "That your boy?" he asked Mike, squinting at Garth."

"He is," Mike lied.

"He's doing a good thing, a very unselfish thing. That's a good boy."

The old woman let go of her husband's arm and stepped over to Garth. To his horror, she reached up and took hold of one of his cheeks, pinching it. "*So* handsome," she said. "I could gobble you up."

"So," Mike chimed in, "about meninosis—"

"You don't need to tell me," the old man said. "I know all about it. It's dreadful. But they *will* find a cure, I'm sure of it. Now, listen." He held up a withered index finger. "You take this and put it toward the cause." With his other hand, he took his wallet from inside his suit coat and extracted a fifty-dollar bill.

Garth's jaw dropped. The old woman thought that was just charming, and pinched his cheek again.

Mike took the bill, deposited it in the fishbowl, and gave the old man a gentle hug as he thanked him.

They spent a total of three hours in front of the grocery store, then relocated to the grand opening of an appliance store a mile away, where the balding, pot-bellied owner seemed more than happy to have them set up in his parking lot beneath the streamers of flags and balloons. The results were the same. Some people ignored them deliberately as if they were nothing more than a nuisance; some dropped a single dollar bill into the bowl, or two or three bills folded together, and a few people—deeply moved, they claimed, by this charitable effort because members of their own families were suffering from similar illnesses—happily handed over ten-dollar bills. And, as it had been at the grocery store, almost any time a lollipop was usurped by a child, the parent shelled out for it.

Only one man gave them trouble: a local doctor who was surprised that he'd never heard of meninosis in all his years of practice and asked a few specific questions.

Garth was at a loss. He had nothing to say about meninosis other than what he'd read in the pamphlet; he swallowed nervously, made the saddest face he could, and spouted, "It's a potentially fatal disease that deforms organs and feet!"

The doctor didn't seemed to be moved. He turned to Mike and asked, "Where's your organization based?"

"California."

"Is there a web site?"

"There is: yourchildandmeninosis.com. Only, it isn't up and running yet. Part of the funds we're raising today will go to the completion and maintenance of the site."

"Huh," the doctor said, sounding skeptical. "Well, I'm a bit befuddled, because one would reasonably assume I'd have come across this disease—at least in a textbook. Do you know anyone who personally *has* it?"

"Yes," Mike said, lowering his voice, "I do." He glanced at Garth. Was he talking about *him*? Is that why Garth was supposed to look so sad? Because he had meninosis? Acting sad was one thing, but acting sick—even for charity work—seemed a little extreme.

He gave a little cough (having no idea whether or not meninosis affected the lungs). The doctor walked over to him. He placed both hands on Garth's shoulders and looked him dead in the eye. "Son," he said, "if you really think you've contracted something—this 'meninosis,' or anything else—you should come see me." He let go of Garth and reached for his wallet. Instead of money, he handed Garth one of his business cards.

Garth glanced at Mike, who gave him a nod both sincere and severe. "Okay," Garth said, taking the card. "Thank you."

"We'll get to the bottom of this, PDQ," the doctor said, then glanced one last time at Mike before walking into the appliance store.

"I think we're done in Hopewell for a while," Mike said. "What do you say we grab a late lunch, then hit Petersburg?"

The day felt foreign, even cinematic. It was as if Garth had watched it happening to someone else rather than to him. Over dinner that night, his mom talked for a while about a particular partner at the law firm who'd been, as she put it, "a pain in the you-know-what" all afternoon because she couldn't get his Excel spreadsheet to print right. "Is it my fault the person who sent it to him didn't bother to set the print area?" she asked. "Is it my fault he won't pay for me to take an Excel training class?"

"It's not," Mike said.

"Anyway, enough about that. I hate complainers. How did you men occupy your time today?"

Garth glanced across the table at Mike.

Without batting an eye, Mike said, "In an educational way, actually. We toured the Museum of the Confederacy."

"Really? That doesn't sound too much up Garth's alley."

"I think he was more fascinated with it than I was— not that I didn't find it fascinating. You weren't bored, were you, Garth?"

"It was pretty interesting," Garth said, barely recognizing the sound of his own voice.

Mike took it a step further. "Sonja, did you know they have the saw they used to take off Stonewall Jackson's arm?"

"Ugh," she said. "I'm sorry I asked."

Mike grinned and offered a slight shrug, then resumed eating.

After dinner, Garth retreated to his room, turned

on his computer, and opened the Wikipedia home page. Suspecting what he was about to find out, he typed *meninosis* into the search box.

Nothing.

He switched over to Google and tried the word there. Same result, except that Google asked if he'd really meant to type *men in noses*.

How surprised was he, really? He'd been a little suspicious from the start, but had believed enough in Mike, so had put those suspicions aside in order to get through the day. *Which says as much about me as it does about Mike,* he thought.

He clicked away from the site, shoved up from his desk, and turned to see Hutch sitting in the doorway to his room, tail wagging and one of his ratty tennis balls in his mouth.

"Sure," Garth said. "I could use a little distraction."

The sun was nearly down and the streetlights were starting to come on. He stood in the backyard and threw the ball for Hutch over and over again, replaying the day in his head.

After a while, Mike came out and stood next to him. He slipped his hands into his pockets and rocked on his heels.

"You feel set for day two?"

Garth threw the ball again and, without looking over, said, "You're a pretty good liar."

"Whoa. That's either an insult or a compliment. You're talking about the Museum of the Confederacy thing?"

"Um, that and the fact that meninosis doesn't exist?"

"It exists," Mike said. "As a concept. As a . . . means."

"That doctor knew."

"Yeah, that was a little sticky. But other than that, the day went pretty well, don't you think? I didn't count it up, but we must have pulled in about five times one of your paychecks."

Hutch brought the ball back. It was filthy and damp with spit. Garth tossed it again. "And how do we get the money to the charity?"

He'd raised his voice a notch with the question, and Mike shushed him and glanced back at the house. "Come on. Cut me a little slack here."

"FedEx?"

"No."

"PayPal?"

"No. There *is* no charity, and I think you've figured that out by now."

"I know. I just wanted to hear you say it."

"Well, if I'd told you that right off the bat, would

you have gone along?"

Garth didn't answer—in part because he wasn't entirely sure the answer would be no.

"Let me remind you of the reason we're doing this," Mike said. "You and your college fund. If we do this for a little while and get it into the bank, it'll only be easier on your mom when it comes time to write out the tuition checks."

"It's illegal."

"Not really. When you get into the technicalities of it, no one who gave us money asked for solid proof, no one asked for a receipt, everyone who gave did so of their own free will."

Hutch was worn out, at last. With the ball in his mouth, he walked a slow circle and then lay down in the middle of the yard, panting. Garth turned and looked at Mike for the first time since he'd come outside. "Right."

"Okay, okay," Mike said, shrugging his shoulders, "*technically* it's illegal, but it's a victimless crime. Think about it. When people give money, they get a warm fuzzy feeling, like they've done their good deed for the day. They feel better about themselves."

"That old man gave you fifty bucks!" Garth hissed.

"People only give what they can comfortably afford,

so the amount is always relative. That man's going to go to bed tonight feeling fifty dollars better about himself. See what I mean? Everybody wins."

"Why did he say he knew about the disease if it doesn't even exist?"

"Because he's a know-it-all. And the best kind of know-it-all is a generous one. Listen, you're not going to get all ethical on me, are you? We're not picking anyone's pockets; they're *giving* us the money. We're helping out your mom, and *your* future."

"I know. I get it. I just don't like the idea of being a 'cause.'"

"We've all got needs." Mike leaned sideways, nudging Garth with his elbow. "And admit it: you got into it after a while, didn't you? Felt a little rush?"

Of course, Mike was right; Garth *had* enjoyed watching money fill the bowl, and after a while he'd even enjoyed the attention he was getting.

His brain slide-showed from the "charity" business to oily Mr. Peterson and the rodent parade. He weighed one against the other.

No contest, if you took ethics out of the equation.

Correction: no contest if you took *guilt* out of the equation.

Addendum: no contest . . . if you were never caught.

"What about Mom?"

"Like we talked about before, this has got to be our secret," Mike told him. "That's the only way it'll work. You get that, right? She'd be totally against the idea."

Garth agreed. In fact, his mom would be mortified if she found out what they were doing, even if—or because—it was all for their benefit.

"I hate to put it so bluntly, but we'll just have to invent a daily roster of fake activities for a little while. And we can't give her the money piecemeal because she'd ask where it was coming from. We'll have to . . . amass it . . . and then give it to her all at once. We'll say we bought a lottery ticket and got lucky."

Garth played out the scenario in his head. "It's a whole nother lie," he said.

"I know. I really do. But sometimes you have to lie to a person in order to help them."

"Which is why you lied to *me*?"

"Exactly. Does that make sense?"

It did and it didn't. He clapped his hands together to rouse Hutch, and the dog lumbered toward them.

"Desperate times," Mike said, "desperate measures."

The next day they worked Colonial Heights, two different locations, and filled the fishbowl two more times.

Garth felt embarrassed one minute, justified the next. Late in the day, he caught himself vying for a person's attention before Mike could, and felt proud when he succeeded.

During the drive home, Mike said, "You did a good job today, by the way."

"Thanks, I guess."

"I'm going to have to come up with something else, though. I can only say the word *meninosis* so many times and keep a straight face, you know?"

Actually, Garth thought, *you could probably say it a billion times, if it brought in a dollar every time you said it.*

And so could I.

Meninosis, meninosis, meninosis.

Ka-ching, ka-ching, ka-ching.

That evening, Mike made up another story about where they'd been (this one involving the Edgar Allan Poe Museum and the Confederate White House), and rattled it off over dinner, peppering in details he'd no doubt gotten out of a guidebook.

Garth retreated to his room as soon as the meal was over, feeling exhausted but exhilarated. And, yes, guilty about having gone along with the lies to his mom.

And yet, he reminded himself as he sat down at his desk, *she's the one who's asked me to live a lie.*

He stared at the HMS *Victory*, its plastic hull, its starchy trapezoids of cloth that would comprise the sails, once the ship was completed.

Don't be an idiot. One lie has nothing to do with the other, and one doesn't justify the other.

Does it?

As if answering this question, an odd buzzing sound emerged from the *Victory*'s hull. The entire ship vibrated—but just slightly. He leaned forward and peered into the opening where two of the deck panels had yet to be glued into place.

A cell phone lay inside.

He saw the caller's number flashing on the little screen. It was *their* number.

Carefully, he extracted the phone, opened it, and said, "Hello?"

"Just a friendly reminder," Mike said. "You have a call to make, right?"

Two days later, at Bone Sweet Bone, Garth told Lisa about finally getting up his nerve to make the call and how Adam was coming over that Thursday to watch the movie. He thought she was going to be happy for him, and she was—for about two seconds. Then he made the mistake of telling her how Mike had prompted him to finally make the call.

"Wait—I don't get it," Lisa said. She was trying to coax Earl, a twelve-year-old whippet, to chase after the squeak toy she'd just bounced across the floor.

"You don't get what?"

"Have I not been encouraging you for months to do something about this?"

"About Adam? I just met him a week ago."

"About peeking your head out of the closet. About calling ROSMY. I'm the one who invited Adam to the river, remember?"

"You know about the situation with my mom—"

"Yes, I know about it because I'm your best friend. That's why I was trying to help you." She gave Earl a gentle tap from behind, but he leaned backward into her hand, his head bowed. "You need exercise," she told the dog. "Stop being so stubborn." She turned back to Garth, who was cleaning Earl's cage. "I've been saying over and over that it wouldn't be the end of the world if you at least made a few gay friends, and maybe even asked one out—and you haven't budged an inch. What special powers of persuasion does 'Mike' have?"

Good question, Garth thought. Was it because Mike was older? Family? Maybe it was because all this encouragement was coming from a guy who was a near-visual replica of his dad. Or maybe it was simply: because he was a *guy*.

Lisa was staring at him, waiting for an answer.

"Why do you always say his name like it has air quotes around it?"

She huffed. "Sometimes he doesn't feel so much like a person as like some . . . force . . . that's taken you over. I don't know. What have you two been up to, anyway?"

"We've been touring the Museum of the Confederacy," he said, sailing Mike's lie and hoping it would float. "He was, you know, curious after we talked about it."

"Huh." She didn't sound convinced. "And what else?"

"Why does it matter *who* persuaded me to call Adam, anyway? Maybe all Mike did was stick the phone in front of me at the right moment. Maybe I persuaded *myself.* Is that a possibility?"

She walked over and picked up the squeak toy, then carried it back to where Earl was cowering. "I'd just like a little credit, is all."

"Okay," he said. "Everyone gets credit. Everyone gets a gold star. Happy?"

She crouched down beside the whippet. Showed him the toy. Tossed it again. The dog didn't move.

"I'm playing fetch with myself," she said—to Garth or the dog. Or both.

Thursday dragged by. Finally, it was evening, and after they'd eaten dinner (pizza—Mike's treat) and his mom had left for her concierge job, Garth set about getting ready. He showered, brushed his teeth, combed and recombed his curly hair, then pulled out a bottle of hair gel he rarely used and mussed it through the mop. The results were ridiculous; his hair looked plastic. After rinsing the gel out in the sink, he applied a smaller amount and tried to shape it—with the help of the hair dryer—into something that looked at least nonfreakish. As a result, he went from plastic to poodle. Then back to plastic. Finally, he shampooed all over again and surrendered to his usual mop.

The jeans were an obvious choice: he owned only one pair that sufficiently masked how skinny his legs were (even though Adam had already seen his legs). As for the rest of the outfit, he laid out across his bed a Penguin polo shirt (repro), a *Star Wars* T-shirt (vintage, from the Salvation Army), and two other T-shirts that were plain but had bright, solid colors. Not enough options, he thought. He added a short-sleeve button-down, then stared at the selection for at least five minutes. Finally, he went into the living room, where Mike was watching television.

"You going topless tonight? That'll definitely send a message."

"Very funny. Can I use your phone again?"

Mike reached into the pocket of his cargo shorts, and held the phone out toward him.

"Thanks."

"I'm proud of you for finally getting your nerve up, by the way. You're not nervous now, are you?"

"Why should I be nervous?" Garth asked, his voice betraying both defensiveness and a slight tremble. He carried the phone back to his room and dialed Lisa's number.

"Hey," he said when she answered, "quick question—"

"Whose phone are you calling from?"

"Mike's. So what shirt do you think I should wear?" He rattled off the selection to her. Because his wardrobe wasn't exactly expansive, she knew all of his clothes by heart.

"This is why you called me?" Lisa asked. "For fashion advice?"

"Yeah."

"The *Star Wars* shirt. Definitely."

"Thanks."

"Good luck."

Barefoot, he stood against the doorjamb and placed his finger against the wood, level with the top of his head, then checked it against the mark he'd made a month ago. He did this every few days, always frustrated, always discouraged. He tried not to extend his spine (which would have been cheating), but tried not to slouch, either. The finger landed on the same mark he'd made nearly six months ago.

Trying not to think about the apparently permanent stagnation in his growth, he examined himself in the mirror that hung on the inside of his closet door. Okay, so his hair looked like crap and his body sort of resembled a toothpick dipped in pancake batter. But things could be worse, right? His gaze drifted further into the mirror and he saw behind him the flotilla of ships and boats.

Plastic models.

Toys.

He was fifteen, and his room could have belonged to a seven-year-old.

Don't freak out, he told himself. *The two of you aren't even going to be in your room. It's going to be you, Mike, and Adam sitting around the living room watching a DVD. With Mike there, that's all it can be. A movie date, end of story. Calm down.*

Stop channeling your mom.

The doorbell rang.

"Want me to get that?" Mike called from the living room.

"No—I'll get it!" Garth hollered. But by the time he'd taken one last glance at his hair in the mirror, tucked and untucked his shirt, and emerged, Mike had already answered the door and Adam was standing in the living room.

"Hey," Garth said.

Adam smiled and gave a little wave.

"Big movie night," Mike said. "Oh—I picked something up for us at the store." He walked into the kitchen, leaving the two of them alone.

"So," Adam said, "having a good week?"

I'm having one of the strangest weeks of my life, thanks

for asking. "Yeah. I've been showing Mike some of the local . . . attractions, I guess you'd say. The Museum of the Confederacy, stuff like that." How easily the lie came now. But never mind. Adam looked fantastic. His loose white T-shirt somehow still managed to accent his chest and show off his arms, which were speckled with fine blond hair. *He's so out of my league,* Garth thought. Though if Lisa were here, she'd probably point out that he didn't *have* a league.

"Garth, can you come in here a minute?" Mike called from the next room.

"Have a seat," Garth told Adam. "I'll be right back."

When he got to the kitchen, Mike was standing at the counter holding a box of popcorn. "Um . . . where's the microwave?"

Garth raised his eyebrows.

"Don't tell me."

"It broke a while back, and we haven't really gotten around to getting a new one."

"Okay, time to improvise." He tossed the box to Garth, dug under the counter, and brought out a large pot and a lid. "Tear one of those open for me, would you?"

"What are you going to do?" Garth asked, opening a package.

Mike dumped the buttered, unpopped kernels into the pot.

"I don't think this stuff works that way."

"Oh ye of little faith." Mike turned the burner on and put the lid in place. "The trick is low, low, low heat, and you can't blink or it'll burn to a crisp. Hey, Adam," he called out, "are you a Coke man, a Sprite man, or a Dr Pepper man?"

"Coke's fine." Adam called back.

Garth winced. "I don't think we have any—"

But Mike nodded toward the fridge and said, "I took care of it."

When he opened the door, Garth found several liters of soda sitting on the shelf. "Thanks."

"My pleasure."

A minute later, he was carrying two large cups into the living room.

Adam was sitting on the couch.

Garth sat down next to him—careful not to sit too close—and handed him his drink.

"Thanks. I hope this film lives up to the endorsement I gave it."

"I'm sure it'll be great."

After a few seconds, they heard the pings of the first kernels hitting the pot lid. "The trick is to keep shaking it!" Mike called out, as if the three of them were having a discussion about his popcorn technique. The television was muted, its glass face filled with helicopter footage of a highway police chase.

"Oh, I hate these shows," Adam said. "The guy trying to get away *always* wipes out after crashing into about a dozen other cars."

"I know. Reality TV must be a director's nightmare."

"No, I mean, what about all those innocent bystanders who got hit and ended up in the hospital, or worse?"

"Oh—right." Garth fumbled for something to say. "And then they show it ten times in a row, at ten different speeds."

"Slower and slower and slower. And, finally, I'm, like, why am I watching this?"

Garth thought about offering to change the channel, but he didn't want to call attention to the fact that they had no cable. Had Adam noticed?

Mike appeared, his own soda in one hand and a large bowl of popcorn in the other. "Who says you need a microwave to make microwave popcorn?" he asked proudly.

Yep, Garth thought. *That's us. No cable, no microwave. Oh, and if you care to look up, you'll see a water stain the shape of Texas.*

Then he remembered that Mike had painted over the stain. The ceiling paint—now covering the primer—nearly matched the surrounding white.

"Smells great," Adam said.

Mike set the bowl down on the coffee table. He scooped up a handful of popcorn, dropped into the armchair, and said, "Is it showtime?"

They weren't ten seconds into the credits—just past the opening scene where a boy is harassed by his classmates and coach on the soccer field—when Mike bolted out of his chair.

"What's wrong?" Garth asked.

He dug his phone out of his pocket and squinted at it. "I have to take this, but keep the movie going; I won't be long." He started off down the hall. "Hello? Lenny! How are you doing?"

"Who's Lenny?" Adam asked.

Garth shrugged. "I have no idea."

Mike closed the door to his room, muting his voice. When he reemerged a minute later, he had his shoes on and was holding his car keys.

Garth hit Pause. "What's up?"

"I have to go meet someone."

"What are you talking about? You don't know anyone here except us."

"Weird coincidence, but this guy I know from

Nevada is in Richmond, and he wants to get together so we can go over some business stuff."

"Business stuff," Garth repeated.

"Yeah. Listen, you guys watch the movie without me, okay? Sorry to bolt like this but, you know, business is business."

He was already headed for the door.

"So where are you meeting this Lenny?" Garth asked, realizing he sounded more like a parent than a nephew. Mike, he suspected, had had this sudden departure planned from the get-go.

"That same restaurant where I took you and your mom. Really, I'll be late if I don't get going, so . . . enjoy the movie, okay? Nice seeing you again." He waved in Adam's direction as he opened the door.

"You, too," Adam said.

Then Mike was gone.

Garth looked at the television screen—a frozen image of a boy climbing a fence—and then glanced cautiously at Adam. "I didn't know he was going to do that."

Adam shrugged.

"I really thought it was going to be, you know, the three of us hanging out," Garth said.

"It doesn't matter. Let's just watch the film."

The movie was as good as Adam had promised

and Garth eventually stopped worrying and let himself get caught up in it. He even forgot about preparing some intelligent remark for when they talked about it afterward—until suddenly the movie was over.

"Well?" Adam asked.

Garth hit the Stop button on the remote. The screen went back to another reality show—this one about a pack of ex-childhood stars shouting at one another. He lowered the volume and said, "It was great. Really great."

"How about that depressing apartment complex where they all lived? It permeated everything, didn't it? A great example of setting functioning as character. And what about that ending? The actress who plays the mom is awesome."

"Yeah," Garth said. "The mom was great."

"So what was your favorite part?"

"Oh. The kiss scene in the woods, I guess."

"Yes! Fantastic shot, right? The way the camera pulls back so that the forest grows around them—like a metaphor for the world they're up against?"

Actually, Garth had just liked the fact that those two cute guys were making out with their bodies pressed together. "Yeah, the symbolism was . . . great."

"And the music is perfect, don't you think? It's kind of ironic when you consider the name of the group."

"Who was it, again?"

"The Mamas and the Papas, which is cool, given that the parents had such a key role in the whole thing. I mean, Ste's dad is obviously an ass who makes his life hell, and Jamie's mom wants to be laid-back but she's worried about him getting pushed around."

An unsettling—and slightly creepy—thought entered his head for the first time. "Hey, did Lisa give you some information packet on me or something?"

"What do you mean?"

"On my . . . situation with my mom," he said. "Did she tell you about that?"

"No. Why?"

"Because the movie is sort of like what I've got going on right now, with my mom. There are similarities, anyway."

"Well, don't worry—there was no information packet. Besides, I picked this off the shelf when we first met, remember? So unless she planted me in the bookstore . . . "

"Never mind. Dumb thought."

"It's not dumb. I think that's just the way it is with gay stories in general. Or gay teen stories, anyway. The parents are mixed in there somewhere, and it's usually not ideal."

"Is it not ideal with you?"

"Ah." Adam shook his head. "With me, it's not my mom who has a problem being laid-back; it's my dad."

"Really?"

"He has this picture in his head, this paint-by-numbers diagram of how a 'man' should live his life. Not for me, thanks. I'd rather choose the colors as I go."

"That's a good way to describe it. So do you and he argue?"

"Well, sometimes we—" Adam stopped himself. "Never mind, scratch all that. I'm being insensitive."

"Why?"

"I shouldn't complain about my dad around you."

"Because mine's dead?"

"Well, yeah," Adam said.

"That doesn't mean you can't complain about *your* dad. Go ahead." It sort of did—but in a way that Garth felt wasn't correct; he couldn't expect people to go through their lives editing themselves around him.

"Okay," Adam said. "So, my dad is sort of like Ste's, in the movie. Not that he drinks or beats me, but he can be an ass. Let's put it that way. And when I'm really honest about it, I can be an ass with him, too, so I guess it's a two-way street. Sorry—I'll shut up now."

"It's *okay*," Garth said.

"Lisa did tell me a little about your dad's accident.

It sounds awful. She said you were so strong through all of it."

"Really? She said that?"

Adam nodded.

Had he been strong? His memory of the weeks following his dad's death were dark and watery; he'd just assumed he'd been a mess. "She was a big help through all that."

"She's crazy about you, you know."

"Yeah?" he said, thinking of how irritated she'd been at the shelter the other day.

"And I can't say I didn't at least *try* to get some info on you, but she wouldn't budge."

"Why?" The idea was embarrassing—but exciting, too.

Adam shrugged. "I was curious. So what *is* this 'situation' with your mom? Unless you don't want to talk about it."

"No, I can talk about it."

He gave Adam a very scaled-down version, feeling only slightly guilty about breaking his promise, and Adam's reaction was similar to Mike's. Only, Adam made a point that Mike hadn't.

"It's kind of a delicate balance, isn't it? For all of us, I mean."

"Who's 'us'? Gay people?"

"Well, also people in general. And families in particular. It's a delicate balance between what you need and what other people need for themselves, you know? Like with my dad. There really aren't any one-way streets."

Garth mulled this over for a moment, trying to decide whether or not he agreed. "I guess."

"Anyway, your uncle seems cool."

"Yeah, I'm still getting to know him, but Mike is pretty great," Garth said. His mind suddenly shifted gears. Had Adam wanted Mike to stick around? So that the evening was the opposite of anything remotely resembling a date? Or was he being paranoid?

"How long is he here for?" Adam asked.

"Another week or two, I guess. He's actually my dad's identical twin."

"That's got to be bizarre."

"Yeah. Sometimes we'll be doing something, and I'll look over at him and it's like this weird glitch, something not quite right with the picture." Garth stopped himself. The image in his head all of a sudden was of him helping his dad's twin scam money from strangers. He felt bad all over again about how easily he'd lied when Adam had asked about his week, remembering how Lisa had mentioned that Adam had "honesty issues."

Adam paused. "Is he gay?"

"Lisa asked the same thing. No, why?"

"He seemed so cool with being in the bookstore with you, so cool with the whole gay thing."

"He's not gay, but he's definitely cool about it."

"Some straight people just *aren't,*" Adam said. "Which is totally Dark Ages thinking. People like my aunt Sadie? When I came out to her, she told me she'd *pray* for me."

"What did you say?"

"I just smiled and said, 'Okay. I'll pray for you, too.'"

"And do you?"

Adam shook his head *no* and faked a slightly baffled expression. "I never seem to get around to it."

This cracked them both up. "Wow," Garth said. "So are you out to everyone you know?"

"Not everyone. I'm out on a need-to-know basis. And, basically, *almost* everybody needs to know, if they're going to *know*-know me." He paused. "You know?"

"No." Garth laughed again. "I mean, yes. But no. It feels so weird—even sitting here talking to you about it. Isn't that pathetic?"

"No, it makes sense."

"The way my mom reacted when I told her . . . "

He wasn't laughing now. "She's made it pretty much impossible for people to know me, and definitely impossible for me to have any gay friends. I wouldn't even know how to *be* around them, or how to act."

"Just be yourself." Adam said. "And, hey—guess what?"

"What?"

"You *do* have a gay friend."

So we're friends, Garth concluded. This hasn't been a date. But what had he been expecting, anyway? Some hot make-out session? Imagining it made him want to kiss Adam on the spot.

"Thanks," he said.

"You're welcome. Um . . . " Adam tilted his head slightly to one side. He seemed to be waiting for Garth to say something. "Tonight's been fun," he finally said, ending the awkward pause himself.

"It has," Garth managed.

"Maybe we can do it again sometime."

"Sure." *Don't leave it at that,* he told himself. *'Sure' is just as bad as 'Whatever.'* "I'd like to do it again. Watch a movie, I mean. A film. With you." Inwardly, he winced at how stupid he sounded. Why couldn't he just relax? Adam was being nice. Everything he'd said had been nice. The expression on his face right now? Nice. And those eyes?

Beyond nice.

Who could take a sentence like "You do have a gay friend" and turn it into something negative?

Garth Rudd, that's who. He cleared his throat as he chose his words. "Well, I don't know how many gay friends *you* have—maybe you're up to your eyeballs in them—but I guess you have one more now."

"Cool," Adam said. His eyebrows bounced once as he smiled.

"Only, don't tell anyone."

They both laughed again—though it didn't really feel funny to Garth. To save face, he clarified, "Lisa, of course."

"Of course."

"But no one else. For now, anyway."

"Got it."

The lock on the front door clicked and Garth's stomach clenched like a fist; his mom was home early from her concierge job, he thought. But, no, it was Mike—holding on to the door and leaning into the living room as if he might have the wrong house. "How are you guys doing?"

"Great."

"How was the movie?"

"Really good," Garth said.

"I was relieved he liked it," Adam added.

Mike nodded and smiled at the two of them.

"So I guess I'll head out now," Adam said. "Thanks again."

Garth watched Adam stand, and he stood, too, and there were good-byes and handshakes and an unexpected hug (for Garth, not Mike), and for a moment the whole evening felt like some kind of audition that Garth might or might not have passed. That seemed to clash, somehow, with Adam's advice that he be himself, because how could you be yourself when you were worried about how well someone else wanted to know you? And why would you want to even *be* that self if it didn't measure up in their eyes?

9

The following Saturday, he was hurriedly slapping a broom over the worn boards of the porch when his mom opened the door. Without stepping outside, she peeked cautiously into the bottom mailbox. "Thank goodness," she said. "No bills. What's your rush?"

"I'm running late," he said. "I'm meeting Lisa, and she'll flip if I keep her waiting. I'm already sort of on her bad side."

"Well, you can always sweep the porch tomorrow. Why are you on Lisa's bad side?"

He paused, cut her a glance, then resumed his slap-dash work. "No reason. She's just in one of her moods."

"Happens to all of us, now and then," she said. "Do you need any spending money, by the way? I know you're in between pay periods, and, knowing you, you're probably depositing your whole check into your bank account."

"I'm fine," he told her.

"Well, let me know if you need any. For movies or whatever. "

"Thanks." He kept his head down, his face burning with guilt.

"Do you want anything from the grocery store?"

"I'm not picky," he said.

"Okay. Remember that the next time I come home with generic Oreos." She disappeared back inside, closing the door behind her.

He was pushing what little dirt he'd amassed over the sides of the porch and onto the grass when he heard a "*Psst*" from the front window. When he turned around and squinted through the screen, he saw Mike squatted down on the other side, peeking beneath the bottom of the half-drawn shade.

"The hawk takes flight by moonlight," Mike said.

"Huh?"

"That's secret agent talk. I have a question for you."

Garth waited, still holding the broom.

"I was thinking about that shelter where you volunteer."

"What about it?"

"Do you think they'd let you borrow a couple of dogs for a day?"

"*Borrow?*"

"Yeah. You know, round up a couple of them and . . . borrow them for a day."

The front door opened again. Garth's mom stood on the threshold, half in and half out of the house, her purse hanging from her shoulder and her grocery list in hand. She was staring down at Mike.

"Why do you want to 'borrow' dogs?" she asked him. "We have Hutch."

"Hutch is great. But I'm a *huge* dog lover," Mike said smoothly. "I'm nuts about them. I shared a Rottweiler with my ex-fiancée, and she got custody when we broke up. I really miss him. I just thought it would be fun to spend some time with some dogs one afternoon. You know, walk them around. Air them out. Take them to one of those dog parks."

"Oh," Garth's mom said. "Why are you crouched down at the window?"

Mike straightened up so that only his knees were visible beneath the shade. Garth imagined him on the other side of the wall, performing some smooth, offhanded shrug. "Just trying to be funny. You making a grocery run? Need some help?"

"No, thank you," his mom said.

"All right. But I'm chipping in a third of the bill later. No arguments."

After she'd left, Mike emerged onto the porch and

gazed up and down Floyd Avenue. "Nice day," he said.

"Uh-huh." Garth squinted at his uncle's watch and leaned the broom up against the front of the house. "So what's this about dogs? Tell me fast because I've got to run."

"Don't let me keep you."

"No, tell me why you asked. Now I'm curious."

"Just what I said." Mike shrugged. "Walk them. Air them out. Give them a little exercise." He glanced sideways at Garth. "Do you have a Scooby-Doo costume in your closet, or did I imagine that?"

The narrow tip of the Fan District (so named because of its shape) ended at Virginia Commonwealth University. The campus was, according to Lisa, a "cornucopia of weirdoes." They hung out there from time to time. For photographic subject matter. For the sake of enriching their exposure to the different walks of life. But really, Garth knew, for the sake of scoping out guys.

This had become a much more pleasurable activity for him now that he was out to her. They would weigh in on who was cute, who was hot, who was too much of a nerd to be attractive, who was just nerdy enough. Mostly, they focused on the skater boys—those sneering, sinewy, scruffy guys who never carried books or backpacks, and who seemed oblivious to the world around them (other than the concrete "waves" they surfed). They would offer Lisa a peace sign, sometimes, if they saw her raise her camera. Or that downward thumb/index finger/pinky stab gesture that meant . . . *This rocks? I rock? Chew on my sneaker?* Garth had no idea. Now and then one of them would raise his middle finger but, as she had with Mudpie, Lisa only found it hilarious and snapped the picture anyway.

For these little adventures, she sometimes wore props that she hoped might make her look older and blend in. Eyeliner (she never wore makeup otherwise). A fake nose ring. Today, her prop was a T-shirt she'd spray-painted herself: black cotton with dripping red letters that formed the word PAWN. She was almost too pretty to look the part, Garth thought, but he didn't say anything.

The two of them were sitting side-by-side on a concrete bench, watching a pack of boys glide, jump, and tumble. The noise of their wheels slamming down over and over again echoed against the walls of the surrounding buildings.

"So, *yes*," she was saying, "there are scholarships I can apply for—and I will because I have to. But thus begins the whoring process."

"The *what*?" Garth asked, laughing.

"I'm serious. The minute you start bowing before the almighty dollar, you become a whore. I don't care whether you're an artist or a politician. Make that first bow, and it's whore, whore, whore." She lifted her digital camera and took a shot of one of the skateborders in midair. "And it's a shame, because I am going to have to *claw* my way into the laps of those New York scholarship-granters so I don't end up here, while the raw truth of the matter is that a true artist"—she touched the camera to her collarbone—"*doesn't need* to be locked away in some lofty arts school tower; she needs to be around *genuine people.*"

"Wait," he said, "I'm confused. Are you saying you *do* want to go to an exclusive arts school or not?"

"I don't know!" Suddenly, she sounded more confused than angry. "I mean, put yourself in my shoes. Do you think you're going to find genuine people at some mondo-competitive school where the student body is made up of whores? No. You're going to find the genuine people *here.* But here is where you *aren't* going to make the necessary contacts to survive in Art World, U.S.A.—so what do you do? Kiss your integrity good-bye and embrace your inner whore."

"You're in a great mood today," he said.

"I'm not. I'm in a rotten mood. I was right about Stacy, by the way."

"Pregnant Stacy?"

"She wants the baby, but she doesn't want my brother. Suddenly, my parents are having second thoughts about paying for the you-know-what."

"Because they want her to marry Jason, or because they don't care about the baby if Stacy doesn't marry him?"

"I think you just answered your own question," Lisa said.

"That is so screwed up. So the Stacy situation has put you in a bad mood?"

"No," she said flatly.

He could have asked her to explain but knew she was going to do it sooner or later, with or without an invitation.

Two of the skateboarders, Garth noticed, had rolled away during her diatribe; three remained. Lisa raised her camera at the remaining three and clicked.

She said, "One of them will be a painter, one of them will be a truck driver, and one of them will kill a man."

"Based on . . . ?"

"I've told you, I'm very intuitive. The tricky part is knowing which is which."

"And how would you 'know' that, for sure?" he asked.

"Observe." Camera in hand, she got up and approached the trio. Zeroing in on the shirtless (and cutest) one, she clicked his picture and began talking to him, but they were too far away for Garth to overhear. The guy started shaking his head almost immediately, moving his oily locks of hair around like seaweed. After a moment, Lisa turned and stomped back to the bench.

"Well, *that* one," she said, sitting down, "is definitely the murderer."

"Why? What did he say?"

"All I did was ask him, 'If you absolutely had to choose one collection of work to be launched into space and preserved forever, which would it be: Warhol's or Barney's?'"

"Who's Barney?"

"Never mind."

"What did he say?"

She huffed and mimicked the skateboarder's voice. "'Who-o-a-a, it's Saturday, lady friend. Class is dismissed.'"

Garth started laughing.

Lisa groaned, but then laughed along with him. "'*Lady friend?*' Come on!"

"All right, explain something to me," Garth said. "Why are you flirting with these guys? You were all psyched about Billy Fillmore the last time I saw you."

"Billy Fillmore is a whore," she declared.

"Come again?"

"He's Mr. I Have a Promising Career in Football and Mr. Worship My Biceps. Hello? No. Could there be a more boring person on Earth? He's already talking about what professional teams he'd be perfect for, and what huge contracts he has coming to him!"

"Well," Garth said with a shrug, "a person has to make a living, right?"

She huffed again. "I told him I was a photographer, and he asked me if I had any naked pictures of myself! Can anyone say *tacky*? Can anyone say *stupid*?"

"Tacky," Garth said. "Stupid."

"And, I swear, he was looking at me like I might have them in my purse, on our date, ready to whip out and show him!"

"But you told him you keep them at home in your dresser, right?"

"I don't *have* any nude pictures of myself!"

"I'm kidding. Speaking of dates," he said, "I had a really good time with Adam the other night."

Lisa glared at him as if he'd insulted her. Then she

opened her mouth, hesitated for a moment, and nailed the real topic like a sledgehammer burying a spike: "*Was* it a date?"

"I—I don't know. It sort of was, and sort of wasn't. We watched a movie—a *film*—and had a good time. I don't think either one of us is hung up on the whole 'date' thing. It's sort of trivial, right?"

"Was the ubiquitous 'Mike' there?"

"*No,*" Garth said. "He was supposed to be, but he left at the last minute, and Adam and I watched the film alone. And talked for a while afterward. He said you told him I was strong."

"I might have," she said, looking down at the cement. Her mind seemed to have gone somewhere else—back to Billy Fillmore, maybe.

"Did you know his aunt is a Christian homophobe?"

"Can I change the subject for a second, and be totally upfront with you?" she asked.

They'd just gotten *on* the subject, but Garth yielded. "Sure."

"I don't buy it that you and your uncle have been touring all these Confederate haunts. I know you hate that stuff, and I heard what he had to say about the topic that day we drove around together, so I think you're lying. Which makes me wonder what's *really* going on. But I won't pry."

Her arms were folded now, her head drooping. Her body was slumped on the concrete bench in the very shape of a crowbar, ready to pry.

"We've just been hanging out. What do you care?"

"I *care*," she said, "because you've stood me up twice since he came to town, and because you're obviously bullshitting me about how you two spend your time, and even though I think there's something totally fishy about him, and even though *I* was the one who put you and Adam in the same place geographically—after your 'magical meeting' in the bookstore, that is—you're giving all the credit to Mike! It really bugs me."

Obviously bullshitting. Lisa hardly ever swore; she thought it was a sign of simple-mindedness. But had he stood her up *twice*? He could only think of the one time since Mike had arrived.

"Oh, and by the way," she added, "when your best friend asks you what's up or what's new, you might mention that you quit your job. That might be something major worth sharing."

"How did you—"

"I went by that skankpit of a department store to say hi since I haven't been seeing much of you lately, and the lady at the register told me you quit."

"I was going to tell you," he stammered. "The thing is, my mom doesn't know."

"Mike knows, though, doesn't he?"

"It's got nothing to do with Mike," he lied.

She picked at a fleck of red spray paint on her T-shirt. "I'm tired of wondering what's going on." She got up from the bench and, without looking back, said, "You can hang out here with your secrets and your pipe dreams."

He watched her approach a pair of rough-looking guys who'd just rolled around the corner of the English building. Pipe dreams? he wondered. About Adam, or about Mike? What the hell was she getting at?

I haven't lied to you, he wanted to call out.

But like so many other things, that wasn't true.

He was alone with his mom that evening. Mike, claiming Saturday night restlessness, had gone out for a burger and a drive. They sat in the living room with the shoe box of photos he'd given them and the new photo album. "I really like this one," his mom said, lifting a snapshot from the pile and holding it up for Garth to see. "Too bad it's damaged."

Garth looked at the snapshot. In it his dad was maybe fifteen, dressed in brown pants and a light-blue windbreaker, hunched down and holding what looked like a peanut for a blurry little shape at the base of a tree. "Is that a squirrel?"

"It must be. Look at how handsome he was. Just like you."

"Yeah?" He'd never before thought there was much resemblance between him and his dad, but he *was* beginning to see a likeness in these photos and was glad to hear his mom thought so, too. "My hair's so much curlier."

"And you hate it, right?"

Garth nodded.

"You know what's funny about that? Your dad always wanted your hair. He said it even when you were a baby."

"Really? I'd have traded with him in a heartbeat."

"The grass is always greener," she said. "You want to include this one?"

"Actually, can I put that one in my wallet? It would be nice to carry around."

"Sure." She handed him the snapshot. Like so many of them it was, as Lisa would have put it, "old school": perfectly square with a white border. One of the corners was bent back, and a crease ran vertically up the middle, causing some of the picture to have flaked away over the years. "Just be careful with it. It's already pretty beaten up."

He set the snapshot to one side, then reached into the pile for another. "Here's a baby shot. Both of them."

Two large, round heads dominated the picture, both smiling. In the background, a white shirt and an anonymous necktie—the chest of whoever was holding them, probably Grandpa Rudd.

"Butterball cheeks," his mom said, and sighed. "We can put that one near the front, if you want."

"Does it make you sad, looking at all these?" he asked.

"Yes and no. How about you?"

He ran his eyes over the pile. "I don't know. I guess not as sad as if they were pictures of *us*. These are like getting a glimpse of the kid I didn't get to know. Does that make sense?"

"It does. To be honest, anytime I think of your dad— not about the accident, but about *him*—it's both happy and sad. They've almost become the same feeling. And I think of him about a thousand times a day."

"Happy and sad rolled up together all the time?"

She was holding another snapshot—this one taken from the front seat of a car, looking into the back, where his dad sat clutching a stuffed penguin. She sank back into the couch and lowered the snapshot to her lap. "I think that's what grief is, when you really love the person who died. That's what I've come to believe, anyway. You miss him a lot, don't you?"

Garth nodded. "Mike and I drove out to the cemetery, the day we went to the mall."

"You did? I didn't know that."

There's a lot you don't know about, he thought. "He wanted to visit the grave. I thought he was going to cry, at one point."

"Well, I'm glad to hear it."

"That we went?"

"That he nearly cried." She set the snapshot back onto the pile, sifted through for another. "Forget I said that."

The remark begged for a follow-up question, but Garth could tell from the expression on her face that she really did want him to forget it. Cautiously, he said, "Mike . . . talked to dad. At the grave."

"People do that."

"I've seen people do it in *movies*," he said. "Not in real life."

"Honey, your dad was very proud of you. You should keep that in mind whenever you're feeling sad."

That was about the *last* thing he wanted to keep in his mind at the moment. His dad wouldn't have been proud of all the lying Garth had been doing lately. Garth slid the picture into the clear plastic sleeve and brushed his hand through the pile, eager to change the subject. "Did Dad and Mike not get along, as grown-ups? There are almost no pictures of the two of them together after, like, seventeen."

His mom glanced toward the front door, as if worried Mike might walk through it at any second. She lowered her voice. "They fought some. The fact is, I think they just turned into very different people. Which is normal. They were twins; they weren't two halves of one thing."

"Except when they were an egg."

"Of course. But who you are as a child, even as a teenager, isn't necessarily who you're going to be as an adult. And you can't be compatible with everyone; that's not realistic."

"Is that how Dad put it? That they weren't compatible?"

"No. That wasn't your dad's style. He would say, 'Mike's got his head in the clouds.' Or 'He's living in a fantasy world where people have no responsibility.' Things like that. He didn't like the fact that they'd grown apart, but he didn't know how to change it."

"So"—he pushed his fingers through the snapshots and found one of his dad and Mike, around ten years old, each holding wrapped presents—"what about you?"

"Me?"

"Do you get along with Mike?"

"What a question," she said. "He's your uncle."

He studied her, waiting for more.

"He's just visiting, anyway. So even if I didn't, it wouldn't be the end of the world."

"That doesn't sound very glowing."

"Don't bait me." She smoothed her hands over her legs and then leaned forward, flipping back a leaf of the album to look at the page they'd just completed. "It was *very* thoughtful of him to give us all these photographs of your dad."

"You still haven't answered my question."

"Well, of course I *get along* with Mike. Do I think he's the most mature man I've ever met? The most levelheaded? No. But he's family." She flipped another page, then another, back to the first one they'd done: a half-dozen baby pictures were anchored behind the plastic. Six pairs of smiling, "butterball-cheeked" infants indistinguishable from each other. "He showed up out of the blue, we welcomed him in, and that's the way it should be. And I'm very thankful for how he's helping out. At the same time"—she glanced toward the door again—"I'm glad he's not sticking around indefinitely."

"Why?"

"Frankly, the more I observe, the more I start to agree with your dad. Which is something you don't ever need to repeat."

"I won't."

"Let's put it this way: he's no role model."

10

Mike stood before Garth's closet, one hand holding a coffee mug and the other extended toward the old Halloween costumes. He looked like someone giving a pitch at a board meeting—save for the fact that he was in a T-shirt, and barefoot. And the idea he was pitching was insane.

"You've got to be kidding me," Garth said.

"Just hear me out. *Cute* equals *money*. If a charity drive—*any* kind of charity drive—gets little kids involved in the actual money-raising, the results double. Triple, sometimes. I know it's a sensitive subject, but you could easily pass for thirteen. And in the right outfit, because of that thing we're not supposed to mention, you could pass for even younger."

"Thanks a lot."

"You're welcome. You should take it as a compliment, you know. When you're forty, you'll probably look twenty-nine."

"I'd die," Garth said. "I'd drop dead on the spot if someone I knew saw me wearing one of those things."

"Which is another reason why we're not doing this in town. And we're not talking about putting you in a diaper or a dress. It's just an old Halloween costume."

"I know, but . . . come on, Mike. Get real."

"I am getting real. I'm getting very real, and I know what I'm talking about. We're doing this to boost up your college fund, remember? To ease the burden on your mom?"

Garth was sitting on the edge of his bed. His body had gone stiff when he'd heard Mike's proposal. Now, as his eyes ran over the costumes, he felt his shoulders droop with a weight that was part surrender, part dread. "Which one?" he asked, though he already knew the answer.

Hutch started barking from the backseat of the Camaro as soon as they emerged from Bone Sweet Bone.

"Okay," Mike said, keeping a firm grip on Mr. Smith's leash, "let's all play nice." Mr. Smith—a midsized, wire-haired mystery breed that'd been at the shelter for nearly six months—was panting and straining at the end of his tether. When he heard Hutch's bark, he began to whine.

Garth was carrying a Scottie-cum-dachshund named Tuva. She squirmed in his arms and struggled to get free, but he knew from experience that she was a zigzagging nightmare to walk. "You're going for a ride," he told the dog, nudging the top of her head with his chin. "A little adventure."

"They're not going to fight, are they?"

"I think they just need to smell each other."

And that's just what they did, thoroughly vacuuming one another's bodies from head to tail once they were all in the backseat. Mr. Smith seemed to take an instant liking to Hutch and settled down to licking the aging spaniel's ear. Tuva, done sniffing, tried to bound over the console into Garth's lap. Garth blocked her with his hand.

"What's he, antisocial?" Mike asked as he backed the car out of the parking space.

"She. And, yeah—sort of. I think she had it in her head she was going to be leader of the pack, but Hutch beat her to the punch by having the home-field advantage *and* making the most noise."

"How can you tell?"

"It's obvious. Now her ego's bruised and she doesn't want to witness their bonding."

Mike pushed his lower lip forward, impressed.

"Wow. You're like a dog shrink."

Tuva's front paws landed on the console again. Garth looked directly into her eyes and touched a finger to her nose. "You are going to fall if you stay like that."

"I'm going to start calling you the Dog Whisperer," Mike said, then turned onto the main road, causing Tuva to flop backward.

Garth reached between the seats and helped her up alongside Mr. Smith. "So what exactly is the 'cause' this time?"

"Helping these poor, disease-ridden animals get the medical treatment they need."

"Uh-huh."

"Hey, I forgot to tell you," Mike said "Adam called this morning while you were in the shower."

"Are you serious? Why'd he call *you*?"

"What can I say? He likes me. He called to talk to you, of course. You still haven't given him your home phone number, have you?"

"He never asked for it."

Mike rolled his eyes.

"What? I didn't want him calling and Mom getting suspicious."

"Suspicious of what? He's a friend; he's calling. There's nothing to be suspicious of."

"I've never done this before—with *any*one," Garth confessed.

"Well, he asked for you, I told him you were in the shower, and he said for you to call him back."

"But how did he get your—"

"It was on his phone from when you called last week. Are you going to ask him on another date?"

They passed a pickup truck with a bumper sticker that read THE SOUTH WILL RISE AGAIN!

"Look at that," Garth said, pointing. "What does it even mean? Rise to what?"

"You're changing the subject."

"I'm not. I mean, I am, but isn't that sick?"

"You sound like your friend. What's her name? The one who doesn't like me."

"Lisa. She doesn't dislike you, she's just very . . . vocal about how she sees the world."

"I understand," Mike said. "'Artists' are historically temperamental."

More air quotes. Garth didn't feel like discussing Lisa with Mike any more than he wanted to discuss Mike with Lisa. They were polar opposites, with Adam running like an equator between them. "I didn't officially ask him out in the first place. *You* asked him over to watch a movie."

"Admit it, you're dying to see him again. And he

wants to see you, too. Do the math."

"I'm bad at math," Garth said. "It's my worst subject."

"You know what? When I was your age, and it was summer, my worst subject was the *last* thing I cared about. I just wanted to have fun."

That said, he gunned the engine, barreling them toward their next destination.

They set up shop in front of a superstore in Gum Springs. Mike unfurled another banner (THE NATHAN MALLARD DOG RESCUE MISSION it read, and below that, in smaller letters, CELEBRATING TEN YEARS OF SAVING PRECIOUS CANINE LIFE), bookended the fishbowl with two Snoopy dolls still bearing their price tags, and laid out another plate of Tootsie Pops. Finally, he took Hutch's and Mr. Smith's leashes from Garth's hands (leaving Garth with Tuva) and tied both dogs to the bike rack next to the table. Mr. Smith took advantage of the proximity and began nuzzling Hutch's neck. Tuva, jealous and riled all over again, panted and strained at the end of her own leash, snapping Garth's arm.

"Who's Nathan Mallard?"

"No idea," Mike said, straightening a fresh stack of pamphlets in front of the fishbowl, "but it sounds authentic, doesn't it?"

"I wouldn't know."

"Sure you would. You're a professional. Speaking of which—time to suit up."

The moment of dread. Garth had his backpack with him, and after a cautious glance around, he hesitantly tugged the zipper open and reached inside.

An hour later—what felt like an eternity when you were dressed in a hooded, pointy-eared Scooby-Doo costume you hadn't worn since you were ten—the bowl was well on its way to being filled with cash.

"In the early stages, the evidence is in the tail," Mike was speak-hollering. "Soreness. Inflammation. Mid-stage, you can see irritation on the bottoms of the paws. But tropolitis does its primary and most debilitating damage to the *joints*. Have you ever seen the joy in a dog's face when it runs? Of course you have. But have you ever seen the sadness, the confusion in the face of a dog that *can't* run? It breaks your heart. That's what these dogs—and many others like them—will have to face without proper professional treatment."

"They look perfectly healthy to me," said a stocky man in a checkered blazer.

"I'm glad to hear it," Mike retorted. "Because they *feel* lousy. If their blood work is any indication, that is." He tried to hand the man a pamphlet.

The man didn't take it. "That one," he said, nodding

toward Garth and winking, "looks fit as a fiddle."

"And so he is. But honestly, sir, there's no joking about tropolitis. We lost two in the past week alone."

"You lost two what?"

"Dogs."

"I hope you find them." The man wandered off into the parking lot.

"Tightwad," Mike muttered. "Notice he didn't even have any shopping bags? Guys like that have got nothing better to do than window-shop and be cynical."

Garth didn't respond. The material of the Scooby-Doo costume was nylon but felt more like plastic; despite the relatively cool day, he was already feeling warm and starting to itch. For better or for worse, Mike had nixed the plastic dog mask, thinking Garth would look more "adorable" with his face showing. Then he'd produced a can of shoe polish from his pocket and blackened the tip of Garth's nose.

"And you're from where?" asked a man with a pony-tail and a goatee.

"The home office is in Shokan, New York, but we have missions in five different states," Mike replied smoothly.

"Shokan's near Woodstock. My sister has a pottery store there."

"Does she? Woodstock's a beautiful town."

"She's an earth lover but an animal hater. I always thought that was kind of a contradiction."

"Seems like it to me. No disrespect toward your sister, of course."

"None taken." The man reached for his wallet.

As he was dropping money into the bowl, a little girl asked, "Can I have one?" She wasn't looking at the dogs; she was looking at the Tootsie Pops.

"Absolutely," Mike told her. "These little guys *want* you to have a lollipop."

The girl reached out and took three. As she stuffed them into her pocket with her right hand (her left hand was clutching a Milky Way), her mom sighed and opened her purse.

And so it went. The banner snapped back and forth in the warm breeze. The dogs sniffed around the asphalt, wagged their tails at anyone who approached the table, and lapped up water from the metal pan Garth had had the foresight to bring from the shelter. Nearly everyone who passed by took notice of the display. Most people lingered to find out a little more. And many of them searched their pockets/wallets/purses/souls and managed to produce some sort of donation. By Mike's count, they'd made over four hundred dollars in the name of meninosis. Garth had no idea how much money tropolitis was bringing in now, but in terms of the attention they were getting, it seemed clear that people's love for sick dogs outweighed their love for sick children.

"You seem a little distracted," Mike commented during a stretch when there was no foot traffic around them.

Garth switched Tuva's leash to his opposite wrist. "What do you mean?"

"You just seem to be someplace else."

I wish. "What do you want me to do?" He glanced down at his brown nylon-clad body. "Bark? Sniff butts?"

"Be *present,* you know?"

"I'm present," Garth waved the hand that wasn't clutching Tuva's leash. "Woof."

"The point isn't to act like a dog. The point is to be—"

"Cute."

Mike steered a finger toward him. "Bingo."

" . . . was his name-o," Garth muttered.

"Here they come."

A family of five had emerged from a Suburban and was approaching the store. The young boys immediately rushed up to the two dogs chained to the bike rack and began fawning over them, while their sister held back. She was around twelve years old and had a sneer set into her face that looked practiced. When her dad stopped at the table and asked Mike about tropolitis, she said, "Oh, please."

Mike launched into his spiel—but he didn't get far before the mom gasped and put her hands up over her ears.

"I hate hearing about suffering," she declared.

"I understand," Mike said. "And these little guys do suffer."

"I can't stand it," the woman declared.

"Neither can I."

The girl renewed her sneer, then asked, "If they're so sick with this gross disease, why not just put them to sleep?"

"Ashley!" her mom snapped. "What have I told you about rudeness?"

"I'm not being rude. I'm just asking."

"Because," Mike said with a set to his own mouth that was half smile, half frown, "with the right treatment, they can live long and fairly comfortable lives. And they can be observed so that we can learn more about their 'gross' disease." He glanced at Garth, as if imploring him to dive in.

"Everyone deserves a chance," Garth said.

"What's on your *nose*?" the girl asked him.

"Shoe polish."

"That's dumb."

"What's *dumb,*" Garth said as Tuva wound her leash around his legs, "is putting a dog to sleep just because it's not in perfect health. How would you like it if you got sick, and then someone killed you instead of giving you medicine?"

"Ha-ha," Mike said, clapping his hands together. "Let's not go overboard."

The dad glanced at his watch. "We've got to get moving if we're going to make it to your sister's place for lunch."

"Okay," the mom said. "Come on, Miss Sass Mouth. Boys, leave those dogs alone."

The five of them continued on into the store. Just as she was passing through the double doors, the girl turned around and stuck her tongue out. Garth stepped free of the lasso Tuva had made and thrust out his own tongue.

With his hands in the pockets of his trousers, Mike strolled over to where he was standing. He gazed at the asphalt for a moment, then said, "Let's review."

"Let's not."

"We're trying to make money."

"I *know.*"

"We're trying to be charming."

"And cute, yeah. I get it."

"So let's keep the conversation steered away from the euthanasia of our potential donors, shall we?"

One town over, adjacent to the food court of a strip mall, a frizzy-haired woman in a white sack dress offered to adopt all three dogs on the spot. "I'm an animal fanatic," she told them. "I have four dogs already. Plus six cats, two cockatiels, and a potbellied pig. All of them are named after presidents." She sat right down on the pebbled cement and corralled Hutch into her lap. "A-look at you. A-look. So old and wise and still a little scruff-a-muffin. I'm going to name you Rutherford B. Hayes."

"Actually," Mike said, "we aren't at liberty to let go of these guys. The cost of their medication and treatment is exorbitant, and it would hardly be fair to any one individual to shoulder the burden—"

"I'm rich," the woman said. Her lipstick, Garth noticed, was purple. Her pale gray eyes were ringed with blue eye shadow and were opened just a fraction too wide, making her look perpetually startled. She hugged Hutch and rocked back and forth. "Dot com money. My husband made a fortune before he and his lover were abducted."

Mike cut Garth a glance. "Abducted?"

"That's right, scruff-a-muffin," she said, as if Hutch

had asked the question. She kissed the top of the dog's head three times. "Carried away by aliens. For experiments."

"I'm sorry to hear that," Mike said.

"I'm not." She raised her head and gave him a wide smile, then motioned for Garth to bring Tuva over. Garth hesitated, then stepped sideways so that Tuva, on her leash, could reach her. "*You*," she told Tuva, pinching one of the dog's ears, "are the scroochiest little mop I've ever laid eyes on. Do you want to come live with me? Be Grover Cleveland?"

"That's very generous on your part," Mike told her. "And your . . . presidential menagerie sounds impressive. But, really, we can't let these dogs go."

"I'll buy them," the woman said. The declaration sounded more like a statement of fact than an offer. "Name your price."

Garth waited for Mike's response. When he heard nothing, he looked over and saw the concentrated, calculating expression on his uncle's face. He was studying the woman, sizing her up.

He seemed to be considering her offer.

"Well?" she asked

"They're not for sale!" Garth blurted out.

The woman smiled at him. "Everything is for sale. Look here." She set Hutch aside, stood up, and opened her purse. To his astonishment, she pulled out a roll of money as big as her fist. "Three dogs: one, two, three," she said, peeling off three hundred-dollar bills.

"Who said anything about a price?" Garth asked.

"Not enough? Four, five, six."

Mike rubbed a hand over his mouth as he stared at the money.

"You're crazy," Garth said.

"I can afford to be," the woman said.

"Why don't you just go to a shelter? You could adopt dogs right and left."

"Because when I see something I like, I want to have it. And I like *these* dogs." She peeled off another hundred.

Garth glared at Mike, who seemed transfixed by the sight of the money. When he spoke again, it wasn't to the woman, but to Garth.

"Of course not Hutch. But the other two . . . ?" He shrugged and glanced down at Tuva and Mr. Smith.

"No!" Garth snapped, not caring if the woman overheard. "What am I supposed to tell Ms. Kessler? That they were abducted by aliens?"

"It happens," the woman said.

"You can't buy these dogs," Garth told her. "Not for any price. I don't know why you'd want them, anyway; they've got meninosis."

"Tropolitis," Mike corrected.

"Whatever. They're not for sale."

The smile never left the woman's face. Her gaze drifted from Mike to Garth, then back to Mike, as if trying to determine whether or not he had veto power.

Mike shrugged again and said, "Sorry, lady. He's calling the shots."

Her blue-ringed eyes made one last drift: to Garth, his blackened nose, the nylon Scooby-Doo ears riding on top of his head. "A dog calling the shots," she said. "And you tell me *I'm* crazy."

A moment later, the money was back in her purse and she was wandering into the food court.

"Today went pretty well," Mike said on their way home from the shelter.

Garth was back in his T-shirt and shorts. Hutch was stretched out across the backseat, glad, it seemed, to have it to himself again.

"I thought we'd at least get *some*thing out of that woman after she waved all that cash around," Mike said. "Didn't you?"

Garth didn't say anything.

"What do you think the chances are that she bumped off her husband and his 'lover'?"

"No idea."

They turned onto Floyd, nearing the apartment. In his peripheral vision Garth saw Mike glance over at him, waiting for more.

After a moment, Mike said, "She was certifiable, wasn't she? I think she actually believed you were a dog. To your credit, I guess—though I have to say your heart didn't seem to be in it."

"My *heart*? I was dressed like Scooby-friggin'-Doo! How the hell was my *heart* supposed to be in it?"

"Yeow. Didn't mean to touch a nerve."

"It's got nothing to do with my nerve! It's embarrassing, Mike. I'm not ten years old, you know? Why don't *you* wear the costume next time?" As soon as he said the words, Garth wanted to take them back; he didn't want there to be a next time.

"No offense, but I'm too big. We're doing this for you and your mom, remember?"

"You keep saying that," Garth muttered. "You actually would have sold them, wouldn't you? Tuva and Mr. Smith?"

"Don't you want them to find good homes?"

"Yes, but they don't belong to you! They belong to the shelter! If anyone should get paid for them, it's Ms. Kessler. She shelled out for their shots and has been putting them up all this time. I wouldn't want them living with that crazy lady, anyway!"

Mike hesitated, then shook his head—a little too vigorously, Garth thought. "No. I wouldn't want that, either. Of course I wouldn't have actually *sold* them. I was just trying to string her along to see if we could get a donation. She obviously had money to burn, and it would have been nice if things had gone a little differently."

Garth didn't feel like being chastised. "How much did we make, anyway?"

"I haven't counted it yet, but I'd say we neared four or five hundred today."

"And where are we keeping all this money?"

"It's safe. I don't think it's a good idea for you to be holding on to it. If your mom found it she'd put a stop to things, pronto."

"I wasn't asking to hold it. I was just asking where it is."

"You trust me, right?" He sighed as he pulled up in front of their building. "Look, I hear the frustration in your voice. I do. So . . . I take it you're not too interested in doing this again tomorrow?"

Garth glared at him.

"Okay, okay. Fine. We'll move on. Tell you what, I've got another idea in the works—just one more, and it should go pretty smoothly. It's genius, in fact. A sure thing. We'll do that, put all the money together, and then tell your mom the lotto ship came in. Hey—" He glanced over again and tapped the end of his nose.

"What does that mean? That we're both on the same page? Because I'm not really feeling very 'same page' at the moment."

"No. It means you've got a little tropolitis on your face."

Garth snatched down the mirrored sun visor, and dragged a hand over the shoe polish.

11

The kitchen radio was tuned to an eighties rock station. His mom was tossing a salad at the counter while Mike, in the middle of one of his stories, made hamburger patties over the sink.

Garth eyed them for a moment, making sure neither one of them seemed on the verge of leaving the kitchen. Then he ducked down the hall to the back of the apartment and slipped into Mike's room.

He didn't feel like asking if he could borrow the cell phone. He didn't feel like hearing any more encouragement—as if, without sufficient nudging from some outside source, he would never in a million years be able to do this on his own.

Draped across the foot of the daybed were the jeans Mike had been wearing earlier. Garth pressed his hands against the pockets and found the phone.

He slipped out onto the porch. Then, just to make sure he was out of earshot, he walked down the steps and followed the sidewalk away from the house.

The number was still tucked into his wallet. He dialed it with his heartbeat thumping against his eardrums.

"Hello?"

"Adam?"

"That's me."

Talk. Articulate. Sound human. "Hi. It's Garth."

"Hey!" The voice sounded so glad to hear from him, he felt himself blush. "How's it going? I was wondering if you were ever going to call me back."

"Oh, yeah, I totally was. I mean, I've been wanting to. I've just been so busy these past few days."

"Yeah? What's up?"

Garth didn't really have anything to follow through with, other than the same lies he'd been feeding his mom and, to lesser effect, Lisa. *Stick to the truth as much as possible,* he told himself. "Oh, I've been spending a lot of time with my uncle. You know . . . going here and there, doing a little of this, a little of that."

God, he sounded like Mike the night he'd first arrived—all that vagueness.

With what sounded like genuine interest, Adam asked, "What's 'a little of this, a little of that'?"

So much for the truth. "Mike's become obsessed with Civil War memorabilia," he heard himself say. "Turns out he's a real American history freak. So we've been going to practically every place you can think of. We even drove out to one of the old plantation houses, and walked a few battleground sites."

Adam then made the conversation twice as awkward—and made Garth feel twice as guilty—by asking questions about the plantation house: How big was it? Was it still in good shape? Did it look like Tara in *Gone with the Wind*? Garth made up as much as he could. As he did, he caught himself glancing up and down the sidewalk and at the windows of the surrounding houses, as if some neighbor might pop out of nowhere and challenge him on this litany of lies.

"Hey," Adam asked, "is it just Mike who's got the Civil War appetite, or are you a secret freak yourself?"

"I'm into it to a certain extent," he lied. "Sort of. I mean, I know a fair amount. So what have *you* been up to?"

"Vegging, mostly. I went back to the river, went to a couple of movies. Oh—and I read this great book called *Easy Riders, Raging Bulls*, all about American filmmaking in the seventies. Also, I'm trying to get the hang of this new editing software. It's a lot trickier than I thought it was going to be."

"You must get a lot done when you're *not* vegging."

"That I do."

"Um—big plans for the weekend?"

"My granddad's driving over from Charlottesville on Saturday. He's a total kook—but in a good way. He's basically a kid who never grew up."

Like Mike, Garth thought. Then: *No, probably not like Mike at all.*

There was a long pause of dead air between them—broken only by a car horn farther down the street.

"Where are you?" Adam asked.

"Outside. I was going for a walk and Mike let me borrow his phone. I keep meaning to tell you the reason I haven't gotten around to giving you my number: we just have the one phone—me and my mom, I mean—and she's on it a lot, she's a total chatterbox. There'd almost be no *point* in giving you the number. We don't have call waiting or voicemail," he added. Lie upon lie upon lie. When was his mom *ever* on the phone—unless it was to talk to his grandmother or to take a call from work? "Anyway"—*Do it,* he told himself, *take the plunge*—"do you maybe want to hang out sometime over the next few days?"

"Yeah," Adam said, "I'd like that. What have you got going on?"

Suddenly, he remembered Mike telling him to keep Saturday open. The next scam, he presumed. The last one. "A bunch of boring old chores," he said.

"But maybe one day next week, after your granddad leaves?"

"Sure. Or Friday evening. You could come over, if you want. We could watch a movie at my place. On my laptop—not the greatest viewing screen, but it's the only way I can watch stuff in my room."

"Friday's great!" Garth said, sounding a little more excited than he'd intended.

"Okay. Ever seen *Chinatown*?"

"I don't think so."

"It's a classic," Adam said. "I own it. I watch it every few months."

"You're not sick of it?"

Adam chuckled. "Actually, I'm due for a fix."

"Sounds good. You can educate me on classic cinema. I only really know crappy cinema."

"Well, I don't know squat about the Civil War, so you can educate me on that. If I get some big studio deal—not—I'll hire you as a consultant."

"Well, that would definitely make you the coolest boss I've ever had."

"Oh, I'd be a monster. I'd scream through clouds of cigar smoke and throw coffee mugs across the set."

"I doubt that." He stood on the sidewalk feeling practically giddy about Friday, and yet the lies—even more so than the humid evening air—made him feel sticky. He glanced at the clock on the phone. Dinner would be ready soon. He asked Adam for his address, told him he had to run, and they said good-bye.

The following afternoon, Mike drove him out to the warehouse district beyond Shockoe Bottom. It was a desolate area; many of the warehouses looked abandoned, their doors padlocked and rusted, their windows broken into shards like mouths of jagged teeth.

"Is this the part where you bump me off?" Garth asked, eyeing one particularly creepy-looking building with a dozen NO TRESPASSING signs bolted to it.

"No. We have greater plans for you, Mr. Bond."

"Like what?"

"Lunch," Mike said, and took the next corner, turning them onto a street so marred with potholes that the Camaro scraped bottom.

Half a jostling block later, they were parked in front of a pale little stucco and shingle building called The Single Slice. A man holding a lit cigarette sat sound asleep on a folding chair in front of the window. A fat, gray cat lay stretched out on the pitched roof, licking one of its paws. "We're *eating* here?" Garth asked.

"Best pizza in town."

"How do you even know about this place?"

"I found it last Saturday night when I was taking

my drive. And I'm kidding, of course; it's not the best pizza. In fact, you probably shouldn't touch anything while we're in here—not with your bare skin, anyway. I'll take you for a proper lunch when we're done."

"But why are we here?"

"The last hurrah? This Saturday?" Mike put the car in park, turned off the engine, and opened his door. "We're going to need some help."

The inside of The Single Slice (a name that made Garth think of a fatal knife wound) was dark and smelled of grease. There were people eating and drinking in a few wooden booths that lined the left-hand wall, and several more slumped over the bar on the opposite side consuming sloppy-looking pizza slices, plates of fries, and cocktails.

"Oh my god," Garth said under his breath. "It's the trash pocket, only for people instead of rats."

"What are you talking about?" Mike said. "A rat would be perfectly happy here." He walked straight into the middle of the place, then sat down at a small table and motioned for Garth to join him.

Garth did, hesitantly easing down into a wooden chair stained with what he could only hope was tomato sauce.

A jukebox in the corner was leaking one of those long-highway-back-to-you songs that seemed to go on forever. In fact, it played three times in a row before a large, hairy man in a Black Sabbath T-shirt emerged from the kitchen and kicked the machine with his boot, prompting the song to switch to something louder though no less upbeat. He asked what they wanted, and before Garth could speak Mike said, "Two Cokes."

"Yup," the man said without looking at them, and walked down to one end of the bar.

The drinks came: two unopened cans, which seemed safe enough. Garth wiped the rim of his can on his T-shirt sleeve, cracked it open, and took a sip. Mike didn't touch his, but kept his eye on the bar. Finally (four revolutions of the current song on the jukebox, by Garth's count), he said, "There she is," and eased back in his chair, smiling.

Garth followed his gaze. A woman had appeared behind the bar—a girl, really: blond and very pretty, in an aqua tube top with matching plastic bracelets. She looked too nice, Garth thought, to be in a place like this. But she seemed capable of holding her own. One of the customers sitting at the bar was trying to set his drink on fire with a cigarette lighter. She pulled a flyswatter from a nail in the wall and smacked him on the hand.

"Damn, Jackie," the man said. His lighter had fallen into his drink. "Look what you made me do!"

"Tough eggs," she said. "It's against the law."

"Suppose you and I go do something legal to-night?"

"Suppose you say something *un*stupid for once in your life, huh? I believe I'd rupture an organ from the shock."

She either winked or semisnarled at the man; Garth couldn't tell which. But she didn't look mad, and neither did he.

Garth looked at Mike, who was watching Jackie. Mike couldn't seem to take his eyes off her, and couldn't get the smile off his face.

"Is she why we're here?" Garth asked.

"She's part of the reason, if I'm worth my weight in character assessment. Listen"—he finally broke his stare, leaning forward to speak low to Garth over the table—"I'm going to invite her to join us, talk to her for a minute. Go along with whatever I say, okay?" He caught Jackie's attention and motioned her toward the empty chair at their table.

To Garth's amazement, she came over and sat down between them.

Mike's grin had broadened into a full-fledged, rarely seen smile. She smiled back to a lesser degree, and said in a friendly but knowing voice, "You two are off your regular path, aren't you?"

"We are," Mike told her. "But we're glad to be here.

Do you remember me from the other night?"

She squinted at him with what almost seemed to be a mocking amount of seriousness. Then her face brightened. "You're Mister Vodka and Tonic minus the vodka!"

"That's me."

"You gave me your card."

"I did."

"And who's this?"

Mike introduced Garth as both his nephew and sidekick.

"Well, well, well," Jackie said. "What brings you back?"

"You," Mike said. "I told you, you're just what I have in mind for this job I'm putting together."

"You told me I *might* be just what you had in mind. You told me you were still looking."

"Either the tonic was going to my head or I'm a fool."

She dropped her gaze to the table, still smiling. "What are you saying?"

Garth looked at Mike. "What *are* you saying?"

Mike ignored him and leaned into Jackie. "The same thing I said before."

"That you're a promoter and a model scout?"

"Yep. And?"

"That I had model looks."

"Specifically . . . "

A little burst of laughter escaped her mouth and she dipped her head to one side. "A perfect nose."

"That's right. And I should have just sealed the deal right then, but like I said, I'm a fool. So you remember what we talked about? The one-day, one-shot-deal job this weekend?"

"Yeah."

"Well, it turns out that that job *could* lead to something else once this drive kicks into full gear, but regardless, the company wants you for Saturday based solely on the head shot you gave me, and that alone says a lot about your potential."

She was blushing, Garth thought, though it wasn't so easy to tell in the bar's dim lights.

"What's it called again?" she asked.

"'Grand Slammin' Wheels for Life.'"

"No, I mean the sickness."

"Lepicarthia. There'll probably be media coverage," Mike told her. "You might end up with your picture in the paper, on top of it all. So what do you say?"

She didn't say anything for a few moments. She was listening to the song, or maybe replaying in her mind all the horrible things Mike had told her about what lepicarthia inflicts on its victims. Or maybe she was just thinking about the sum of money he'd told her she'd earn.

"All right," she said, "I'll do it."

"Aces," Mike told her. "Saturday at ten sharp, okay?"

"Okay," she said.

"I'll be back in just a few minutes, you two," Mike said, then got up from the table and strolled casually down to the last booth, where a man with slicked-back hair and a bloated, tomato-red face sat hunched over a mug of beer and a shot glass.

The man barely looked up when Mike sat down across from him. But Mike started talking to him in a low voice, the sound drowned out by the jukebox, and before long the man was rocking back and forth and nodding his head yes.

Jackie was looking at Garth with wide, polite eyes. Garth felt almost frightened, sitting next to her. But of what? Not anything she was going to do to him, certainly. Maybe frightened of what Mike had in store for her. Frightened of how mortified he'd feel if he were taking part in a scam that would rope in this stranger.

If? Who am I kidding?

He shoved a smile onto his face.

"You're one lucky guy to have an uncle like that," she said.

He swallowed. He felt himself nodding with nothing to say, and forced himself to speak. "He's . . . unique, all right."

"One of a kind. He helps out a lot of people, from what he tells me. A lot of girls who move on to bigger things, bigger places. He told me you've been interning with him this summer," Jackie said.

Yes, I've been interning at the School for Young Hucksters, under the tutelage of headmaster Mike Rudd. What do you have to do to get in, you ask? Be in the wrong place at the wrong time. And have no spine whatsoever. Oh, and if you can manage it, check your conscience at the door.

Mike came back to the table where Garth was scissoring his knees up and down and pushing dents into his Coke can.

"Who's that guy?" Garth asked, glancing at the man in the booth.

"Nobody," Mike said, and to Jackie, "Till Saturday." He shook her hand, then turned it over, brought it to his lips, and kissed it.

She laughed and said, "Till Saturday."

Garth pushed up from his chair, glad to be leaving The Single Slice and hoping never to lay eyes on it again.

"So," he said when they were back in the car, "what exactly are we doing on Saturday?"

"Don't worry about it. This one's going to be a piece of cake. What's happening on the Adam front?"

"I'm going over to his place tomorrow night. We're going to watch *Chinatown*."

"That's great!"

"Yeah. I guess I'll just tell Mom I'm hanging out with a friend."

"Sounds like a plan," Mike said, and then he slipped into a bad Chinese accent. "'Bad for glass, bad for glass.'"

Whatever that meant. "Adam told me it's a classic."

"It is, most definitely. Classic. So how about that Jackie? I know you bat for the other team, but if you didn't, she'd be worth stepping up to the plate for, huh?"

"Sure," Garth muttered. He was already regretting that their paths had crossed with hers, and he caught himself wondering, as the warm breeze swirled around inside the car, what his summer might have been like if Mike had never decided to peel off I-95 at the Richmond exit that evening that felt so long ago.

12

After dinner the next evening, he got up from the table, stretched, and announced that he was going over to Lisa's to "hang out."

Mike wiped his napkin over his mouth and winked at him. His mom—who, thankfully, hadn't seen the wink—glanced at the clock on the wall. "Don't stay out too late."

"It's summer," he reminded her. "It's Friday."

"I still don't want you staying out till all hours."

"If I stayed out till 'all hours,' it would mean I never came home."

"And sarcasm will keep you from walking out the front door in the first place."

Mike leaned back in his chair, watching the two of them.

"Well, give me a cutoff time, then," Garth said. "So I know when to be home by."

She looked at the clock again. "Eleven."

"How about midnight?"

"We're not negotiating. I'm the parent." But she seemed to think about it for a moment and countered, "Eleven thirty."

"Eleven thirty," he repeated. "Deal."

"It's amazing, isn't it?" Mike said. "How teenagers can do nothing for hours at a time? I can't imagine how a person could occupy himself just sitting around doing nothing."

"I think you can," Garth's mom told him.

Score one for Mom, Garth thought, and walked out of the kitchen before anything else could be said.

In his room, he threw on a T-shirt, and ran a brush through his hair. He'd decided his motto for the evening was "Expect nothing." If he obsessed over his appearance, it would be a surefire method of guaranteeing that Adam wouldn't care at all.

Expect nothing, and the evening just might have a chance at surprising them both.

The tip of the weaselly little man's knife blade slid just a quarter of an inch up one of Jake Gittes's nostrils. Garth braced himself, sitting next to Adam on the bed. Then the hand pulled away and took the knife with it, and a ribbon of blood sprayed from Jake Gittes's nose.

"*Ooohhh!*" Garth's entire body jerked and he

brought his hands to his eyes to try to block the image. "Ow! Ouch!"

Laughing, Adam made a playful grab for his nose. "Now you've seen the most famous nostril-cutting scene in American cinema."

"Okay." Garth turned his head away from the laptop, which sat on the bed just beyond their feet. "Tell me there's no more . . . splicing and dicing . . . and I'll be fine."

"No more, I promise. Car chases and gunfire, yes. But no more splicing."

"Thank you."

The bedroom—slightly larger than Garth's—had two windows that looked out over Colonial Street, but Adam had drawn the shades. The sun was down now, and the flickering computer screen was the room's only illumination. Garth's eyes roamed the walls, hungry for details about Adam. There were snapshots stuck into the frame of the dresser mirror, but they were too far away to see clearly. A bookcase filled with books and DVD's, but he couldn't make out any of the titles. On one side of the closet hung a poster for a film called *Blue* (that much he could read), and on the other side was a poster for *The Piano*.

Someone tapped on the door, which was pulled to but not latched.

"Come in," Adam said, pausing the movie.

Mr. Walters stuck his head into the room. He was a trim, stern-looking man who, when he'd met Garth earlier that evening, had pumped his hand vigorously and looked him squarely in the eye as if the two of them were about to make a business deal. According to Adam, his dad took himself and most every other topic on earth extremely seriously. There were deep creases in his forehead to prove it, and his hair—the same blond as Adam's—was thinning at the crown.

"Everything okay in here?" Mr. Walters asked.

"Yeah," Adam said. "We're great."

"I thought I heard someone yell."

"That was Garth, hollering in solidarity with Jack Nicholson's nose."

"Ah." Mr. Walters smiled for a fraction of a second; then his expression leveled off, and he glanced around the room as if taking inventory. "Your mom has a migraine. She's gone to bed early."

"Okay."

"Open or closed?" he asked, moving the door back and forth a few inches.

"Closed, I guess, if Mom's in bed. We don't want to disturb her."

"Good thinking." Mr. Walters pulled his head back into the hall and eased the door shut behind him.

"Should we finish the movie some other time?" Garth asked, lowering his voice and motioning toward the laptop. "If your mom has gone to bed . . ."

"No, no, it's fine," Adam said. "I can translate for you. My dad didn't knock on the door because you yelled; he knocked on the door to see what we were doing."

"Because . . ."

"Because he thinks it's what he's supposed to do, as a dad. Check in. Eyeball the place. Make sure we're not in here doing drugs or starting a cult. And the thing about my mom having a migraine? That means they had an argument. Not a knockdown, drag-out—they never have those, thankfully—but they had some kind of spat. So he's in the living room getting his crime show fix, and she's in their bedroom, which is as far away from him as she can get and still be in the house. She's probably reading or watching television in there, but either way, we won't disturb her."

"Okay," Garth said hesitantly.

"And the whole 'open or closed' thing was his way of saying, 'It's okay that you, my unfortunately gay son, have your unfortunately gay friend over, but just know that I know it and that I'm generously—and unfortunately—allowing it.'"

"Wow."

"Honestly. He wants credit for not having a problem

with who I am, even if he does sort of have a problem with it."

"So should I . . . not be here?"

"No! You should. There are a lot of games with my dad. A lot of little signals the rest of the world is supposed to get and process and respond to accordingly. It's part of what my parents argue about: my mom gets sick of trying to guess what he wants and misreading his signals."

"You don't seem to have any trouble reading them!"

"Yeah, well, I think *my* problem is that I read too much into them." He waved the topic away. "Sorry. I'll stop complaining about my dad now."

"I told you, it doesn't bother me. I'd probably have complaints about my dad, if he were still around. Do you guys ever talk about . . . you?"

"You mean, do we talk about my being gay?"

Garth nodded.

"Twice, I think. No, make that three times. The time I came out to them, the time I brought it up again . . . oh, and the time I brought it up again. I think he wants a medal for not having disowned me, but if I never mentioned it again from now till the day I died, he'd be *very* happy. Thankfully, my mom's not so skittish about it."

"Like mine is."

"Your mom's not seeing the situation in a new light, with your uncle around?"

"Um, no. She didn't even like the fact that I came out to him. And she still doesn't know he took me to the bookstore."

"Sorry to be blunt, but that sucks. I sort of thought having such a cool, open-minded guy in the house might have an effect on her."

If anything, she seems a little more worried than normal, Garth thought, *and with good reason.*

They turned back to the movie. Jake Gittes was now glaring at Evelyn Mulwray, half his face hidden behind a large white bandage. Just by his eyes alone you could tell he was thoroughly unhappy. "And Mrs. Mulwray, I damned near lost my nose," he sneered. "And I like it. I like breathing through it."

"Great movie, by the way," Garth said. "Sorry—I mean, film."

"You can call it a movie. I'm not a snob."

"How about 'cinema'? Do people still say that with a straight face?"

"Yes, but that's the place where they *show* the movies. And the talkies. And the picture shows. We'll have you up to speed in no time."

Somewhere between the appearance of the bandage

and the "bad for glass" line Mike had quoted the previous day, their shoulders touched against the headboard—just barely—and remained that way. Garth wasn't sure exactly when the moment had occurred and was thankful that he hadn't noticed when it had, because if watching an actor's nose get make-believe knifed had made him flinch, touching his shoulder to Adam's, on Adam's bed, in Adam's semidarkened room, surely would have been enough to make him jump a foot in the air.

The Los Angeles sky brightened their faces momentarily; then night fell over the screen once again, and the beautiful old cars rolled through the dusk into Chinatown. For as hard as he tried, Garth couldn't follow the story line; it just couldn't compete with his proximity to this incredibly hot guy.

Did I touch you or did you touch me?

Are we even on the same page here?

IS THIS A DATE?

He was afraid to move. He ached to know. Suddenly, the prolonged blare of a car horn filled the room, and then Jake was pulling Evelyn Mulwray off the steering wheel, and Evelyn Mulwray had a hole in her head big enough for one of Mr. Peterson's rats to crawl into.

"*That* doesn't make you flinch?" Adam asked him incredulously.

"Actually, no," Garth said. "Maybe because they didn't actually show her getting shot."

"Forget about it, Jake. It's Chinatown," a man said, and Garth realized the film was ending.

He relished the connection between their shoulders an instant longer. Then Adam broke it, leaning forward to stop the DVD.

Abruptly, the room became twice as dark as it had been. The window shades glowed from the light of the streetlamps. Adam's light blue T-shirt seemed to glow as well. With one hand, he opened up his iTunes and scrolled down through a list of songs; with the other, he rubbed at the back of his neck.

Garth watched him from behind. The sudden silence felt awkward.

But then Adam made his selection, and a drum was struck—faintly, as if from a great distance—and a bagpipe leaked out of the tiny speakers. A singer's voice, raspy and yet somehow smooth, joined the instruments, encircling and drawing them in. Completing them. The combination was beautiful.

When Adam turned around, he moved directly in front of Garth and kissed him.

For a moment, Garth thought there'd been some mistake. How was it possible that Adam wanted to do this at least as badly as he did—maybe even more so, if he was bold enough to instigate it?

The hand Adam had been using to rub his own neck circled Garth's now and cupped the back of Garth's head.

". . . *Please talk to me*," the singer breathed, "*won't you please talk to me.*"

When they drew apart, Adam looked as surprised as Garth felt.

"I have to admit, I'm proud of myself," he said through a little laugh.

"Yeah?"

"Well, I wasn't sure if I was going to be brave enough, and I wasn't really sure if you wanted to . . . "

"Are you serious? It's all I've been thinking about for the last hour. The last *week*."

"Well"—Adam cleared his throat and dipped his head sheepishly—"I'm just glad one of us had a little experience to contribute. It helped, I think."

"Yeah," Garth said, suddenly embarrassed. "Thanks for that."

Adam blinked. "I was thanking *you*. I've never kissed anyone before."

"Come on!"

"You mean you haven't either?"

"Never! I thought *you* would have, because Lisa mentioned you'd dated someone—" Garth stopped himself. *Great strategy*, he thought. *Bring up the ex.*

"Yeah, well—no. We never actually kissed. That's how far *that* got."

Garth glanced over at the laptop and saw that the screen saver had come on: a shifting spiral of colors against a sea of black, like some new life-form that couldn't decide what shape to take. Adam's hand, he noticed, was no longer on the back of his head; it was on the mattress, the fingers softly drumming against the bedspread. "I really liked that song," Garth said. He took hold of the hand, lifted it, and put it back where it had been. "Can we listen to it again?"

His mom was in bed when he got home. Mike was stretched out on the couch, watching an old black-and-white movie on television. Hutch lay beside him, sound asleep. Without moving his head, Mike lifted his arm and brought his watch up to his face. "Missed it by ten minutes."

"Missed what?"

"Your curfew. Don't worry—your secret's safe with me."

"Thanks." Garth started across the room.

"Whoa, whoa, whoa, where are you running off to?"

He glanced toward his mom's closed door, then whispered, "Bed. I'm tired."

"Tired, huh? So were you profitable tonight with you-know-who?"

"Profitable?" he repeated. "You're asking me if I was profitable?"

"Yeah. You know." Mike lowered his own voice to something that was almost a growl. "Did you make ogress-pray on your ate-day?"

Garth didn't feel like talking about it. That surprised him, because walking home from Adam's house, it had been all he could do not to tell strangers on the street how great his evening had been. If he'd had Hutch with him, he would have chatted the dog's ear off with details—about how he and Adam had made out for the length of the entire album they were listening to, about how they had plans to get together again on Wednesday, after Adam's granddad left. But suddenly he didn't want to share the night's events with anyone. Or, he didn't want to share them with Mike. The date (he was confident enough now to at least *think* the term) felt like a very private thing. It felt personal, and to just brag about it to his uncle—the way he'd overheard guys at school brag about the girls they'd gone out with—felt . . . wrong. "We had a good time."

"You watched the movie."

"We watched the movie."

"And?"

He was standing next to the television, his keys in his hand. "We talked."

"*And?*"

Garth just looked at him and offered a shrug.

"Come on," Mike said. "I'm not asking for a laundry list of your carnal activities. I'm just your cheering section here. Did you at least get to second base?"

"I don't know what the bases are. I was never too good at sports."

"All right, crankmeister. I can see you're in a grand mood. Why don't you sit down and watch some of this with me? It's *Double Indemnity*—remember that book I was reading when I first got here? I told you they made it into a movie about a million years ago? This is it. I know Barbara Stanwyck doesn't float your boat, but Fred MacMurray might do something for you. He tells the whole story with a knife wound in his gut, bleeding from beginning to end."

Garth looked at the television. A baggy-faced man dressed in a trench coat and a fedora was approaching a blond woman in a grocery store aisle. "No thanks. Let Hutch out before you go to bed, will you?" he said, palming his keys.

"Fine. Abandon me. I'll get by somehow."

I'm sure you will, Garth thought.

13

His mom was at the table sipping coffee and staring at the newspaper when he walked into the kitchen the next morning. Without thinking, he took a mug from the dish drain and filled it. "Hi," he said, the word stretching into a yawn.

"Since when you do you drink coffee whenever you want to? It's not Sunday."

"Oops. My bad." He removed the top of the pot and dumped the coffee back in, then rinsed the mug out and poured himself some orange juice instead. "You're working today?"

"I picked up some extra hours at the hotel. One of the women I work with, Gina, is finally starting her maternity leave, so I put in for some of her shifts. Time and a half."

"Don't wear yourself out," he said, and yawned again.

"Thank you for your concern." She turned the paper

over, glanced at the back of it, and then rolled it up and tapped it against the table as if she were contemplating whacking him over the head.

"What? It's orange juice."

"How was your evening?" she asked pointedly.

"It was fine."

"Lisa called here."

He felt the muscles in his face tighten. He gulped down a mouthful of juice, dragged his hand over his lips, and said, "Did she?"

The newspaper tap-tap-tapped against the table. "I was a little surprised, of course, because I thought you were at her house."

"I thought I was going to be there, too. I had a change of plans at the last minute."

"I asked her," his mom went on, "'Isn't Garth with you?' She said no, and when I asked if she knew where you were, she said she didn't have the slightest idea and that I should ask your uncle."

Thanks, Lisa. "She's jealous of Mike," he said a little too loudly. "Isn't that dumb? She's my friend; he's my uncle. Why should she be jealous of *him*?"

"Where were you?"

"With a—a different friend. Maybe *that's* why she was jealous. Jealousy eats some people up, have you ever noticed that? It's pathetic."

"Garth."

"Yeah?"

"I want to know who you were with, and why you lied to me."

His mind raced. For a fleeting second, he considered telling her. Adam could just be a friend, right? A guy he met at school, someone he hadn't mentioned before, but still just a friend. They'd sat around and watched a movie. Was that a crime?

"Billy Strickland," he blurted out.

"Billy Strickland?"

"Yeah. I was at Billy's."

She didn't look convinced. "I can't remember the last time you even mentioned him. How is Billy?"

"Same old." The only guy in school who was proud of being able to belch the entire alphabet. Garth couldn't stand him. Why, out of all the names that were floating around in his head, had he come up with Billy Strickland?

Because Billy was the last friend his mom would have suspected him of having a crush on, that was why. Not that she'd ever laid eyes on Adam, but if he'd said Adam's name, she would have asked about him, and Garth didn't want that topic hanging between them like a piñata ready to be burst open.

He did the only thing he could think to do: he

grabbed his mental shovel and dug himself down another foot. "I really don't want you to run yourself down with all these extra shifts, Mom. I can always ask Mr. Peterson for more hours."

"I'm running late," she said. "I was waiting for you to get up so I could hear what you had to say, and now that I have, I need to get to work."

"What do you mean? I told you where I was. I just had a change of plans, that's all."

"We'll talk more tonight." She let go of the newspaper and pushed up from the table, reaching for her purse.

"Mom—"

"I don't have time, Garth. Especially not for lies."

"I'm *not* lying! I was with Billy Strickland!"

"And I was with the King of Prussia. We'll talk this evening when I get home."

The "King of Prussia" had slipped into his room while they were talking. After his mom had left for work, Garth slinked to the back of the apartment—angry at both himself and her, and worried about what lay in store for him that night—only to find a swath of blue and red fabric draped over his desk chair.

Superman. Halloween, circa the sixth grade.

Mike appeared in the doorway.

"What's this?" Garth asked.

He rested a hand on the doorjamb right over the top of Garth's height mark. "I just want to make sure it still fits before we leave the house."

Garth looked at the costume. He looked at his uncle. "No."

"What do you mean? This is it, last time, I promise."

"I'm not in the mood."

"That's ridiculous. I'll bet you're in the mood to make money, aren't you? I'll bet you're in the mood to rake in some cash. Believe me, the dog gig was much more successful *because* of the costume."

"I don't know if this makes sense to you or not, but I just don't feel like dressing up in the Superman costume I wore when I was *eleven*. It's humiliating!"

"It's a step up from Scooby-Doo. Who doesn't love Superman? He's faster than a speeding bullet, more powerful than—" He paused, and examined Garth with what almost seemed to be respect. "You made a home run last night, didn't you?"

"This doesn't have anything to do with last night." (Somehow, it did.) "I'm just saying I'm not in the mood, okay?"

"This is our swan song," Mike pleaded. "Our last hand. Our . . . finest hour."

Garth rolled his eyes.

"I saw that. Seriously, this is *it*. After today, we'll retire, and before long I'll be gone and you'll be longing for the days when I was around and it was the Mike and Garth Show. Trust me. Would you just try the thing on so we know whether or not it still fits?"

Was he persuasive or just persistent? Garth couldn't tell anymore. There was something so eager, so hungry about Mike; he really and truly seemed to *like* what they were doing—to such an extent that pulling the plug on him was nearly impossible.

The costume fit. The legs rode a little high and hugged his calves, but otherwise it was fine. Mike even tried to hard-sell him by commenting that he probably looked better in it *now*, with a little muscle on him, than he had when he was eleven. But Garth ignored him, pulled the costume off, and shoved it into his backpack.

Outside, Mike walked straight past the Camaro and unlocked the driver's door of what looked to be a brand-new Firebird. It was cinnamon-colored, and spotless.

"What's this?" Garth asked.

"Rental."

"What do we need a different car for?"

"Because even *my* wheels aren't slick enough for

today's operation. Get in."

Garth slumped in the passenger's seat as they rolled down the street. He was truly *over* this. And though he couldn't have said exactly why, it *was* somehow connected to last night. To the progress he'd made with Adam. It wasn't that scamming conflicted with Adam, but that *this* Garth conflicted somehow with *that* Garth. But Mike was the guy who'd made both those Garths possible. "I have no idea what lepra-whatever-you-call-it is supposed to be," he said. "And I don't feel like making up a bunch of phony details. *Or* pretending I have it. Just so you know."

"Lepicarthia. Boy, for someone who had what I can only *assume* was a hot date last night, you sure woke up on the wrong side of the bed. The beauty of the lepicarthia idea, if I do say so myself, is that lepicarthia doesn't matter. No one's going to care, because their eyes are going to be on the prize. Well, the prize, and the ornament on top of the prize."

He pulled a manila folder from in between the console and the driver's seat. When he flipped it open in his lap, there was Jackie's 8½ x 11 head shot: her bright eyes and broad smile, her hair teased up into twice the volume it had had the other day. Mike turned the photo over and squinted at the information on the back. He handed it to Garth. "What's that say?"

Garth started to read it to him, beginning with Jackie's eye and hair color.

"Just the address. The rest I've got memorized."

She lived less than ten minutes away, though her neighborhood had a far different—and rougher—feel to it than the Fan District. When they pulled up in front of the clapboard house, Mike tapped the horn.

The screen door opened and a skinny young man stepped out onto the little square of front porch. He had a narrow face and a shock of white-blond hair, and he was clutching something small and black in one hand.

"Jeez Louise," Mike said. "Is he armed?"

"Um, no, that's a remote. They're legal in Richmond, as long as you have a permit."

The door swung open again and Jackie appeared. She was dressed in a tight pair of acid-washed jean shorts and a billowy brown blouse that didn't quite cover her stomach. A tote bag was slung over one shoulder. She practically skipped down the cement steps to the street, where the Firebird sat idling.

Watching her approach, Mike sighed under his breath, "Hel-lo, beautiful."

Garth switched to the backseat. Jackie poked her head into the car, offered them each a cheery "Hello!" and then tried to coax Garth back into the front. "I can sit back there," she said. "I can! Really, I don't need much space. Come on out of there, now."

"We *want* you to sit up front," Mike said. "It's like the head of the table, the seat of honor."

"Wow." She dropped into the bucket seat. "Look at me! Seat of honor!"

"What I want to know," Mike said, "is, could you be any prettier on this gorgeous day?"

"Maybe." She turned around and smiled at Garth. "You're a gentleman to let me sit up here. That was megasweet."

"Everything he knows, he learned from me," Mike said.

"Seriously," she told Garth, "those manners will take you far with the ladies—just make sure they've got enough class to appreciate them."

Garth smiled weakly and thanked her for the advice.

Mike sank his foot down onto the gas.

She lit a cigarette, held it outside of the car, and talked incessantly: about how backstabbing the modeling business could be; about her slimy, flirtatious boss at The Single Slice; about her boyfriend, who worked as a security guard and had the day off but who didn't want to come out to watch her work, which had irked her, but she'd already forgiven him because "only losers stay mad."

"He doesn't like the fair, anyway," Jackie said. "He says it's a breeding pool for pickpockets because he lost his wallet there once. But I really think that's what happened—he lost it. Nobody put their hand in his pocket, I'd bet five dollars on it."

"We're going to the state fair?" Garth asked.

"Yep," Mike said.

"The one at the fairgrounds?"

"Is there another one I don't know about?"

"The state fair," Jackie breathed excitedly. "Prime exposure!"

"That's right," Mike said. "Prime exposure. As soon as we make a little pit stop."

The fairgrounds were on the outskirts of town but weren't exactly in a remote location, as the other scam sites had been. Garth pictured himself dressed in the Superman costume and Lisa appearing out of nowhere. Spotting him. Lifting her camera. *Click.*

Was there *any* possibility of aborting his involvement at this point? He could fake a stomachache or a sudden flu, maybe, demand to be driven back home. He could fake a heart attack or narcolepsy or . . . lepicarthia.

Jackie turned around again and smiled into the backseat. "This whole deal just feels magical," she told

Garth. "You know what I mean?"

"S-sort of," he offered.

"One minute I'm pouring drinks at The Single Slice, and the next minute my career's got a fresh start. I'm just so thankful!"

"We're thankful. Aren't we, Garth?"

He clutched his backpack to his stomach and stared out the side window. *Just one more time,* he thought. *Our last hand. Our finest hour.*

Right.

Mike pulled onto the shoulder of the road just outside the fairgrounds. "Hold tight while I do a little installation," he said, and then reached beneath the seat and brought out a pair of glossy, corrugated placards that read WIN ME! in bright blue letters. He pulled a stubby screwdriver from the glove compartment, got out, and replaced both the front and back license plates.

The parking area was less than half full. He steered them into the middle of the lot and parked diagonally across three spaces. "We'll set up here," he said. When he turned off the engine and opened his door, they heard an ice cream truck song emanating from the other side of a tall chain-link fence. The song was "Pop Goes the Weasel."

"We're not going in?" Jackie asked.

"No cars allowed in there, unfortunately," Mike told her. "And it's all about the car. And you, of course." He glanced at Garth in the rearview mirror and said, "You know the drill."

They set up the card table and the banner poles. True to Mike's word, this time around the scam didn't seem to have much to do with the "cause." There were pamphlets describing lepicarthia, but it wasn't even mentioned on the banner Mike unfurled and affixed to the polls. SOMEONE WILL DRIVE THIS CAR HOME TODAY!, it read. $5 PER TICKET! Next to the fishbowl, he placed a box of ballpoint pens.

Garth took the Superman costume from his backpack and pulled it on over his shorts and T-shirt. He was stepping back into the sneakers Mike had bought him when a hand tapped his shoulder.

He spun around. Jackie was standing next to him on the asphalt, wearing nothing but a pale blue bikini and a pair of low-heeled pumps. She'd pulled her hair up into ponytails that sprang out from either side of her head. "Tell me the truth," she said. "Do I look trashy?"

"No. You look nice."

"Like I said, you're a gentleman. I knew you'd be honest."

"Would you, um, tie me?" He gathered his cape

248 •

out of the way, turned his back to her, and she tied the straps at the neck of his costume.

"You look nice, too," she said.

"I look like a joke. I wore this for Halloween when I was eleven and can still fit into it now."

"That doesn't make you a joke. It just makes you small."

He groaned. "You're right. What makes me a joke is the fact that I'm willing to put it on."

"You're doing it to help sick people. That sounds like something Superman would do, if you ask me."

"So." Mike closed the trunk, pulled off his sunglasses, and froze when he saw Jackie in her swimsuit. "Yeowza."

"What's wrong?" she asked, looking down at herself.

"Nothing. Absolutely nothing." He lifted a large double roll of raffle tickets and wagged it at them. "Let's get the show rolling. You're next to the table," he told Garth, then turned to Jackie. "And you're on the car—assuming it's had a chance to cool down."

"*On* the car? I thought I was going to be *in* the car."

"Well, you can be in it if you want to, but you'll draw more attention, you'll get more . . . exposure out here, where people can see you."

"That's true."

"Just lose the shoes."

She stepped out of the pumps, tossed them through the open window into the backseat, and walked around to the hood, which she scooted up onto backward.

"That's the spirit," Mike encouraged her. He glanced at Garth. "How about you? Feeling the spirit?"

Garth just blinked at him.

"Okay, you both know how a raffle works. People write their names and phone numbers on the companion tickets, and then at four o'clock we draw a name, end of story. It's pretty simple."

The costume itched and was tight under the armpits. Plucking at it, Garth felt his irritation simmer. "But the foundation," he said, "the one in need of funding, so they can research lepicarthia—they're willing to just give away a car in order to raise money? That doesn't really seem cost-effective, does it?"

Mike darted his eyes from Jackie to Garth. "How it works," he said carefully, "is that the good people at Pontiac have *donated* this car to the cause. Could you make a little effort to look like a superhero?"

"What are *you* supposed to look like?" Garth asked.

"The man in charge." Mike scooped a few pamphlets off the stack and turned toward the people crossing the

250 •

parking lot, headed for the fair. His voice kicked into its professional volume. "Five dollars, folks! One ticket! You'll help out a good cause and might drive this beautiful baby home today!"

He didn't drop their money into the fishbowl but kept it in various rolls in the pockets of his trousers. The fishbowl slowly filled up with companion raffle tickets. During a lag when not many people were passing by, he tore off a long ribbon of tickets and tied them in a loose knot around Jackie's bare shoulders.

"That makes it look like they're going to win *me*!" she observed.

"Whatever gets their attention," Mike said.

She laughed. She repositioned her legs, renewed her smile, and waved at a family crossing the parking area. "Help fight the cause!" she hollered. "Get a free Firebird!"

Garth fanned himself with a pamphlet and, prodded by Mike's stare, heard himself saying things like "Make a difference!" and "Change the world!" He felt more than ridiculous. He felt resentful, and ashamed. And, he realized as he stared out at the small crowd, he felt angry. How could he be the same person who'd walked home on air last night? At what point did he become such a contradiction? And who was he more angry at—Mike or himself? "Spend five bucks and feel better about yourself!" he hollered.

Mike walked right over to him and muttered, "Knock it off," then returned to his position on the other side of the table.

Jackie scanned the steady flow of people and speculated on who might be with the newspaper, who might be a magazine bigwig, and who (wouldn't it just be the coolest?) might be a scout for the Fashion Network.

And so it went. The fishbowl slowly filled with tickets. Mike's pockets bulged with cash. He bought them hotdogs and sodas for lunch, but Garth couldn't bear the thought of eating. As the sun beat down, "Pop Goes the Weasel" played over and over and over again, each note like a finger tapping against his brain.

At long last they were nearing raffle time when he heard someone say, "Look, up in the sky! It's a bird! It's a plane!"

He couldn't keep the sneer from curling his upper lip as he turned toward the voice. *Shut the hell up and buy a ticket,* he wanted to respond—but there, standing next to a stooped, gray-haired man wearing a VIRGINIA IS FOR LOVERS T-shirt, was Adam.

14

Garth opened his mouth, but no words would come. What was there to say, after all?

Great to see you. How do you like my cape?

Forgot to mention, I'm a superhero on the weekends.

Do these tights make my legs look thin?

The gray-haired man was smiling playfully, as if Garth were an adorable little trick-or-treater on his doorstep. Adam was smiling, too. He said, "And I thought you were just a mild-mannered animal lover."

"Hey, hey, hey!" Mike called out. He'd spotted Adam and was crossing in front of the table, leading with his hand. "It's great to see you again!"

Adam shook his hand. "You, too." He turned to the gray-haired man. "Granddad, this is my friend Garth and his uncle, Mike." And to them: "This is my granddad, Mr. Varick."

"Call me Jim," his granddad said.

"Mike Rudd," Mike said, and pumped Mr. Varick's

hand. "Great shirt, by the way."

"Thank you." Mr. Varick glanced down at the slogan. "I've lived in Virginia my entire life, and I'm still waiting to find out if it's true. They're keeping that one a secret from me."

"Ha-ha. Me, too, I'm sorry to say."

"Who's your Vanna White?"

"That's Jackie."

Jackie flashed her teeth and waved from the hood of the car.

"You folks heading into the fair?" Mike asked.

"We're on our way out," Mr. Varick said. "My bones are rattled. Adam forced me to go on the Scrambler *and* the Tilt-a-Whirl—twice each."

"It was your idea," Adam said.

"Oh, that's right." His granddad snapped his fingers.

Adam turned to Garth. "This is what you call 'boring old chores'?" He didn't sound like he was challenging Garth; he actually sounded impressed.

"What's the charity?" Mr. Varick asked. He'd taken one of the pamphlets off the stack and was examining it.

Mike jumped on the question. "Lepicarthia. Ever heard of it?"

"I haven't, but that doesn't mean anything. My wife, rest her soul, used to accuse me of living in a bubble. This is probably just one of those things that never penetrated it. Nice to see some people are out doing good in the world while the rest of us goof off." He turned to Adam. "Isn't that right, Mr. I-Insist-on-Riding-the-Giant-Slide?"

"*You* were the one who insisted on the giant slide."

Mr. Varick snapped his fingers. "Oh, that's right."

Adam leaned into Garth and said in a low voice, "It's great to see you, by the way. Last night was . . . amazing."

"Thanks. I mean, yeah, I had a really great time, too."

"And you should have just told me this is what you were going to be doing today. I think it's really cool."

Garth couldn't help himself. He shook his head—just barely—and said, "No, it's not."

"What time's the raffle?" Mr. Varick asked, dropping the pamphlet back onto the table.

Mike shot his arm out and looked at his watch. "In about fifteen minutes. You folks could still get in just under the wire, if you want."

The older man dug out his wallet, selected a ten-dollar bill, and asked for two tickets. Mike handed them over, along with a ballpoint pen, instructing him to write his name on the back of each one.

Watching the exchange, Garth felt an uneasy

churning in his stomach and he felt queasy all over again.

Adam reached over and tugged on his cape. "You look miserable, Superman," he teased.

"I am."

Then Adam leaned in so close that Garth felt his breath against his ear. "What I meant to say is, you *seem* miserable. You actually *look* pretty cute."

But at the moment, *cute* didn't cut it. *Cute* was for puppies and stuffed animals. You didn't want to make out with *cute*; you wanted to pat it on the head.

Adam just smiled at him and said, "Let me do my part for the cause, too." He reached into one of his pockets and produced a five-dollar bill.

"Don't," Garth said, his face burning.

"I can't resist. Every charity should have you working for it. The world's problems would be solved in, like, a week." He extended the money in Mike's direction.

"Don't," Garth said again—to both Adam and Mike.

But they ignored him. The money went from Adam's hand to Mike's, and then down the rabbit hole of Mike's pocket so quickly it might have vanished into thin air. "Good man," Mike said, and spun the roll. "Have an extra ticket, on me."

Garth fantasized once again about faking a heart attack. But the raffle was about to take place, and

Adam and Mr. Varick were sticking around.

Be still, my beating heart, he thought. *Still as in a heart attack. Kill me.*

By four o'clock, most people who'd purchased tickets and filled in their names and addresses had gone on their way: into the fair or home. About two dozen had decided to stay for the actual drawing. Mike looked at his watch, clapped his hands together to draw everyone's attention, and announced that it was, at last, "giveaway time!" He carried the fishbowl over to Jackie, who seemed to have given up on being discovered as a model for the day and was stretched out on the hood as if she might take nap.

"Would you do us the honors?" Mike asked.

"Me?" she asked, sitting upright. "I get to pick?"

"Please."

She reached into the bowl, swam her hand around for a few moments while mugging for the small crowd, and produced a ticket. Mike snatched it from her before she had a chance to look at it, then made a great display of looking at it himself, holding it first at arm's length and then right up close to his nose.

"Zero-zero-two-seven-six-eight-five!" he called out.

Several people in the small crowd sighed with disappointment.

Mr. Varick squinted at each of his tickets. "I guess Lady Luck's not smiling upon me today." He glanced at Adam. "How about you?"

"Me, either. But I've never won anything in my life, so I'm not surprised."

Mike repeated the number, then turned the ticket over and read the name out loud. "Lester O'Neil?"

A raspy voice suddenly boomed over the parking lot: "Lester O'Neil! Lester O'Neil! That's me!!"

A portly, red-faced man in sunglasses and a baseball cap pushed between two bystanders and waved his arms in the air. "That's me!" he hollered again, and lumbered toward the Firebird.

"We have a winner!" Mike announced with excitement.

A few people clapped. Most of them were already starting to walk away.

"My baby." The portly man had reached the front of the car now and was bent forward, caressing the grill with his thick hands.

"Hurray!" Jackie cheered, and smacked her hands together. But a moment later she wasn't clapping. She was staring at the man, *peering* at him suspiciously.

"Congratulations to Mr. O'Neil!" Mike said to the crowd.

"Well," Mr. Varick said to Adam, "let's head out.

Maybe Lady Ice Cream will smile at us on the way home."

"Sounds good." Adam stuffed his worthless ticket into his pocket and turned to Garth. "Too bad you can't come with us."

"Yeah," Garth said. "Believe me, I wish I could."

"Call me, okay? And I'll see you on Wednesday."

"I will."

Jackie scooted forward a few inches, reached out with one bare foot, and tipped the baseball cap off the man's head. "Marcus," she snapped, "what are you doing here?"

"Winning a sports car," Mr. O'Neil/Marcus told her. "What about you?"

Jackie looked from him to Mike, back and forth a few times. "He's one of my customers," she said to Mike. "You were talking to him the other day."

"I was?" Mike asked.

"At the bar where I work. I saw you talking to him."

"I don't recall ever seeing this man before."

Adam, Garth noticed when he chanced a look over his shoulder, had stopped walking and appeared confused. Mr. Varick also looked to be confused. In fact, every one of the dozen or so people still lingering in the vicinity had the same befuddled expression on their faces—except for Jackie, who looked angry.

"You don't even have a license," Jackie told Marcus. "You can't win a car!"

"I can, too!" Marcus spat. "I won it fair and square!"

"Then where's your ticket?"

"I don't need a ticket! Ask *him*!" He pointed toward Mike.

"All I did was pick a name," Mike said, palms raised.

"This man is a low-down creep," Jackie told him. "He's one of my customers. I caught him with his hand in my tip jar a month ago." She looked down at Marcus again. "You can't just pop up out of the woodwork like some . . . *muppet* . . . and drive this car away! There are people who gave good money to charity and one of them deserves to win it fair and square!"

"Okay, folks, show's over!" Mike piped up. "Thanks for being here. Thanks for giving, and thanks for caring." He shot Garth a look and stirred a finger in the air as if to say, *Let's wrap this up.*

But Marcus just glared at the lot of them, raised a wide fist and brought it down on the hood, producing a loud, metallic *whump.*

"Wow," Adam said from several feet away.

When the fist landed a second time, Mike grabbed Marcus by the shoulder and spun him around. "Back off!"

"You said this car's mine!"

"I did *not*," Mike hissed. "I said show up, get fifty bucks and cab fare back to the city. How could you have misunderstood that? Why would I just give you a car, you stupid hick?!"

"Methinks something stinks in Denmark," Mr. Varick remarked.

Adam glanced at his granddad, then at Garth.

"I can explain," Garth said. But he couldn't.

There was a prolonged moment where Marcus just blinked in the warm air, his face as red as cranberry juice. Then he launched forward, head-first.

Mike deflected him, shoving him sideways in a manner that sent him sprawling into Garth's path. When Garth attempted to jump out of the way, Marcus grappled for something to keep himself upright. That something was Garth's cape—which tore away from the costume with a sharp tug at his neck. The man hit the pavement hard, still clutching the fabric and looking like a felled matador.

"I think every one of them's stewed," said one of the remaining spectators.

Jackie was scooting off the hood. "I am not *stewed*, mister!"

Mike jerked open the driver's door, hollered, "In the car! Both of you!" and ducked behind the wheel.

They left everything behind: the card table, the fishbowl, the banner and poles. Jackie no longer had any interest in the "seat of honor." She'd climbed into the back, leaving the front for Garth, who buried his hands in his face as they sped away from the fairgrounds.

"Marcus is a creep, I already knew that," Jackie said, anger fueling her voice, "but now I'm thinking you're just a creep of a different kind."

"I'm not a creep," Mike protested. "I'm a struggling businessman."

"And what's your business, exactly? Being a creep?"

"Don't say that. You had a good time today, didn't you? You enjoyed all the attention, sitting up there feeling pretty."

Garth slumped miserably in the front seat. His neck stung from the cape's having been torn free— as if someone had halfheartedly tried to strangle him. He would never be able to look Adam in the eye again. That was a very bad thing, since in the big picture the two of them would surely run into each other at school next year, and in the small picture (which somehow felt much larger than the big picture), he wanted to do nothing more than be alone with Adam, making out with him as they'd done less than twenty-four hours ago.

Mike had helped make so much possible in his life, and just as swiftly he'd ruined it. He might as well have helped Garth find a new face and then immediately cut off the nose.

And, like Jake Gittes in *Chinatown*, Garth liked his nose. He liked breathing through it.

"What are we doing *here*?" Jackie demanded when they rolled to a stop in front of his house on Floyd Avenue. "This isn't where I live."

"It's where *we* live," Mike told her. He sounded exhausted. "I'm getting your pay for today, because I forgot to bring the cash with me this morning. I'm assuming you don't want it all in fives and ones."

"I don't want your stinkin' money, period," Jackie snapped.

"You don't want two hundred dollars, tax free." Mike didn't make it a question but a statement.

"It's stolen."

"It's not *this* money I'm paying you," he said, tapping one of his stuffed pockets. "It's money I already had before today."

"For all I know, you stole *that* money, too. I don't want it."

"Well, that's just dumb. I'm trying to give you cold, hard cash you didn't have to work your tail off for in that hole-in-the-wall."

She leaned forward and tapped Garth's shoulder, addressing him for the first time since they'd peeled out of the fairgrounds. He was dressed in his T-shirt and shorts now, the damaged costume at his feet (he'd slithered out of it as quickly as she'd slithered back into her clothes). "How about you? Did you know all this was fake?"

The look on his face answered her question just fine.

She huffed and said to Mike. "I tell you what, and this may be the worst thing of all—worse than stealing a dollar here and there. I think you've corrupted this boy."

"Would you just take it easy?" Mike told her. "Really. A good, deep breath right now would do you wonders."

"You didn't offer it to me like what it was," she said. "You lied."

"If I'd offered it to you 'like it was,' you wouldn't have done it."

"I wish I hadn't. I wish I'd never laid eyes on you!"

"Well, since I can't turn back time, what do you want me to do about it now?"

"Why don't you just apologize to her?" Garth suggested.

Mike glared at him.

"Just say you're sorry for lying."

"Both of you," Mike said, "breathe, and give your mouths a rest."

"Let me out," Jackie said.

"Would you just sit tight? I'll go inside and get your pay, then drive you home. *Or*—assuming you're not furious with me beyond belief—I'll take you to dinner somewhere."

"Dinner?" Her mouth hung open for a moment and she gaped at him. "Who's stupid now?"

"Come on." He quoted her from earlier in the day: "'Only losers stay mad.'"

Garth opened his door, got out, and pushed the bucket seat forward. She all but clawed her way free of the Firebird. A moment later, she poked her head back in through the open window. "Maybe I was wrong."

"Thank you," Mike groaned.

"Maybe you *haven't* corrupted this boy totally. *Yet*," she clarified.

Her footsteps clopped up the sidewalk, matching the pounding in Garth's chest.

He left the costume in the car and walked into the apartment, heading directly to his room. Hutch followed him, and when he collapsed on his bed, the dog jumped up and lay down beside him.

"*What?*" he asked the dog. "Stop staring at me."

Hutch held his soupy gaze another moment and then rattled his head, adjusting his collar.

"I wish I were you. My biggest worry of the day would be how my collar fit."

He closed his eyes. Before long, he heard a light knock on the door.

"I'm sleeping," he lied.

"You are not. Can I come in?"

"No."

"I think we should touch base about today before your mom gets home. You know, compare notes."

Compare notes? he thought, staring up at ceiling. *Okay, here are mine, Mike: You've messed up the one really good thing I thought I had going. Or, rather, you've helped me mess it up. Without you I probably never would have actually met this guy, and without you I wouldn't want to die right now from humiliation. Thanks a lot.*

"I returned the rental car," Mike said. And then, af-

266 •

ter a moment of silence: "Listen, I know it was weird, and I know Adam was there for the worst of it. It stinks, I get it. To be honest, I wouldn't want to be seen by my potential . . . dating person . . . dressed like that, either. But you can throw all those costumes out now, you know? You're done with them. No more. I promised you that, and I'll stick to what I said."

Who cared about the stupid costumes at this point? Talking about them to help improve the situation was like sticking a Band-Aid on a severed jugular vein. Mike, he knew, was just worried that Garth would spill the specifics to his mom—a worry that had nothing to do with Garth and everything to do with Mike.

"Would you say something?" Mike asked through the door. "Are you upset, or just tired?"

"Both," Garth called out. "But don't worry—I won't tell Mom about how wearing one of my old Halloween costumes to scam money nearly got my head torn off."

There was a long pause—broken only by Hutch rattling his head again to adjust his collar.

"Okay," Mike said. "Thanks for that. I appreciate it."

H onesty.

He wanted it. He craved it.

He could barely remember what it was.

Feeling so full of secrets and lies that he was either going to throw up or explode, he dragged himself to Lisa's house, sat with her in her room, and told her everything.

She listened to the whole spiraling confession with a look on her face that was a perfect mixture of shock and disappointment. "How could you?" she asked when he was finished.

"I've been asking myself the same thing for the past couple of days."

"How could you kidnap two dogs from the shelter?"

Garth exhaled in frustration. "That's not exactly the worst thing I just told you."

"And Hutch!" Lisa said. She was squatting down beside her desk, repeatedly pushing a button on her printer. "Hutch is, what, eleven? That's like taking an old man out of a nursing home and making him hold up a liquor store!"

"Nobody held up anything. The dogs didn't even know what was going on."

"You're better than that, Garth." The power light on the printer came on, but as soon as she sat down in her desk chair, it went off again. "You care about animals more than that—or, at least, you did before this jerk showed up."

"I still care about animals! I care about a lot of things."

"Really? So, you care about dogs but you've been exploiting them. And you care about your mom, but you've been lying to her about everything."

"Only so that we can put money into my college fund."

He'd started off sitting cross-legged at the foot of her bed. Halfway through the confession, his entire body had drawn up into a tight, uncomfortable knot. Now that it was all out of him the knot felt like it had been untied, but the sensation was hardly liberating; he felt more like a bundle of dirty laundry that had spilled onto her bed. He stretched out flat on his back and let his head hang over the foot of the mattress.

"Why didn't you just tell me what was going on?" Lisa was upside down from this perspective, making fists and gritting her teeth at the printer. She looked in-sane.

"Because *not* telling you—and avoiding you—was easier than hearing you tell me how wrong it was. You have to admit, you can be pretty harsh."

"You've been helping that jerk steal from people! You've been helping him commit crimes! Of *course* I would have been harsh!"

"Judgmental, I mean."

"I'm not judgmental. I have opinions." She fiddled with the cable, and the printer turned on again. "Yes. Thank you," she said to the machine. "Now stay that way and print something, for a change." She highlighted a file on the computer screen and double-clicked on it. The cursor turned into an hourglass as she sat back and brushed her long hair away from her face with both hands. She watched him watching her.

He reached beneath him and dug his wallet out of his back pocket. "Look at this," he said, extracting the beat-up snapshot of his dad attempting to feed the squirrel. He held it out for her to see.

She glanced at it. "So?"

"It's my dad. It's a great picture, isn't it? Mike gave us a whole box of old photos of him and my dad from when they were kids."

"Have you totally lost touch with reality? Why are

you showing me this now?"

"Because it's a great picture. Because I'd give a lung to change the subject. Because I want to die."

"Too bad. You're alive, we're here, and you brought all this up."

"I know. And I owe you an apology."

"For?"

He looked her directly in the eye. "Well, for lying to you."

"And for pulling away? Because you have, you know. I really thought I'd been replaced."

"And for pulling away, yes. God, I feel so . . . awful now. I feel unfixable."

"Don't do that. You don't get to be mopey, all of a sudden. And what do you mean, unfixable? You're not *broken,* Garth. You just did something really, really dumb and wrong."

He rubbed at the dampness on his eyes and then looked directly at her—hard. "What do you get out of knowing me? I mean, why would you still even want to be my friend?"

"What do I *get*? Why would you even ask me that? I get a friend who's a guy who lets me be *me*. Who *likes* me—for me. Do you know why I go through so many boyfriends? They all want me to be somebody else. Some softer, gooier version of who I really am.

All those guys? With the exception of Taylor Pruitt? *They* dump *me*, okay? *I* dumped Taylor Pruitt because he had chronic bad breath. Like someone stuffed a pork chop into a sneaker."

"You never told me that before."

"About Taylor's breath? Oh my god, the *worst*."

"About guys breaking up with you."

"Well, why would I? It's not exactly something I'm proud of. But my point is that I don't get the you-need-to-change thing from you. *And*"—she held out both her hands in frustration, her fingers spread open wide as if she wanted to strangle the air between them—"I *like* you, Garth. You're a good guy—if we erase the past few weeks. And we've logged some significant time together. I like being around you, okay? I like *me* when I'm around you. If I could wave a magic wand and make you straight—and make me attracted to you—I would. But I can't. So you're my best friend."

"You're not attracted to me?" he asked, mustering the closest thing to humor he could manage at the moment.

"Sorry," she said. "You've got Sufjan's sensitivity, but you'd have to pour that into, say, Billy Fillmore's body for it to really click with me."

He almost felt like laughing. Almost. "What am I going to do?"

"About your mom? Never, ever in a million years let her find out what you've been up to with your uncle."

"Really? I thought you were going to recommend full disclosure again."

"Earth to Criminal Behavior Boy: No way. You've been breaking the law. Think she's hyperworried now? Run that past her and she'll have a meltdown."

"That's sort of what I was thinking."

"As for Adam—"

"Him I don't need advice on. I'm just going to crawl into a hole and die. That should take care of things."

"Or you could try and explain it to him."

"*What?*"

"Tell him you were drawn in by your uncle's over-powering charm." She glanced sideways and darted her tongue out as if trying to free it from a bad taste. "Tell him you felt like you had no choice and you've learned your lesson. Trust me, it'll only make you more interesting. You two will bond over it. As for the jerk—"

"Stop calling him that, okay? He's still my uncle."

"He can be your uncle and a jerk at the same time. That's physically possible. As for *him,* my advice is to never have anything to do with him again. Please tell me he dangled a watch in front of your face and put you in some Patty Hearst trance, and that's why you went along with all this."

"I made my own choices," Garth said glumly.

"Yes, but you were seduced, too."

"That's disgusting. He's a relative. He's my dad's identical twin, for god's sake."

"I don't mean it that way, pervert. I mean that, for some reason I can't fathom, you were seduced by his personality, his charm."

"I guess I was. But, you know, aside from all the scamming and lying and humiliation . . . " He realized how pathetic he sounded.

"Keep going," she said.

"It's been kind of nice having him around. I mean, I really miss my dad, and—"

"There is a world—a *galaxy*—of difference between those two men, Garth. And if you even for a second want to justify your involvement with Mike by saying he's a substitute for your dad, you've sold yourself on the biggest scam of all."

"All right! Enough."

"And what makes you think it's over, anyway?" she added.

"Mike said so. We've officially retired. No more scams."

"Or maybe there's one more in the works."

"Nope. Not as far as I'm concerned, anyway. Mike knows how I feel."

She brushed her hair away from her face again and clucked her tongue. "Where's the money?"

"He's been holding it for us."

"Till—"

"Till we're done. Which we are. So I guess he's holding it till now. Ish."

"And you're comfortable with that?"

"Don't be so negative."

"I'm not negative," she said. "I observe the world around me, and I form my opinions. They may sound negative—and they may come out like judgments—but that's only because I'm that very rare combination of both artist and realist."

The hourglass on the computer screen went away. The printer came to life, and a sheet of photo paper emerged inch by inch and dropped onto the tray. "Yay!" she exclaimed, and held it up for Garth to see.

Mudpie was staring him down, scowling, her middle finger dominating the foreground.

If he was honest with himself, Lisa's implication wasn't earth-shattering. It had occurred to him that Mike might be planning something underhanded (or under the underhandedness). But he didn't want it to be true.

His mom was at work when he got back to the

apartment. Mike was washing dishes. "Big guy!" he said, rinsing a plate in the sink. "Where'd you go? I was going to cook us a nice lunch but I got too hungry waiting for you."

"I went for a walk," Garth said. "Just to, you know, think."

"Oh. Want me to make you a sandwich?"

"No, thanks. Listen, I need to ask you something."

"Sounds serious," Mike said. "Let's go sit down."

He led the way into the living room, where Hutch was stretched out in the armchair. Garth noticed what looked like a large shirt box wrapped in Christmas paper sitting on the end table next to the sofa.

"What's that?"

"Sorry," Mike said, "it was the only paper I could find—in the hall closet, behind the coats. It's just a small token of appreciation for everything you've done since I got here. I know I'm not the easiest guy to put up with."

"Thanks," he said hesitantly. "I'll open it later, if that's okay."

Mike sat down on the couch. "You'll never guess what it is, and I'm not going to tell you. You couldn't torture it out of me. And I warn you, the suspense is going to be deadly."

Garth nodded. He settled in alongside the sleeping

Hutch and said, "Thanks," again.

"All right, it's a model of the *Flying Dutchman*. They didn't even carry it at the hobby shop; I had to special-order it. It looks really cool—and very complicated. *Maybe* a ten out of ten, on your scale."

Garth glanced with newfound interest at the box wrapped in repeating, smiling snowmen. But he was in no mood to receive a present—least of all from Mike. He reached down absently and stroked Hutch's head.

"So, you wanted to ask me a question?" Mike asked.

"I've realized something," Garth said. "A couple of things. A lot of things, really." *Coward,* he thought. *Spit it out.* "I'm really mad at myself. And I'm really mad at you."

Mike blinked and focused his eyes on the opposite wall. Drawing his gaze back in to Garth, he said, "*That's* not a question."

"No, but I needed to tell you that first."

"I gathered. You barely spoke to me yesterday."

"And I want to tell you *why* I'm mad," Garth said, "because I don't really think you know."

"I'm all ears."

"What we've been doing is wrong. Like, awful— horrible—wrong."

"Okay," Mike said.

"Don't just say okay. Tell me you agree. Or tell me you think it's normal for an uncle and his nephew to be scamming innocent people in the name of fake charities, lying through our teeth—"

"Wait, wait, wait." Mike waved his hand in front of him. "In the first place, there are no innocent people. And in the second place, while the uncle/nephew aspect of our little operation may be . . . refreshingly unorthodox, let's say . . . the actual act itself is as old as the hills. Believe me, since the first two men stood upright, side by side, people have been greasing palms, picking pockets, and selling the Brooklyn Bridge to one another. It's one of the facts of life that keeps it all interesting."

Garth wasn't in the mood for The Philosophy of Mike 101. "I think it was awful, what you did to Jackie on Saturday."

"Awful. I offered to pay her. You heard me."

"She thought we were the real deal, when it came to the charity. She took you at your word."

"Well, stupid her."

"*Stupid her?* If everybody were *smart,* by that logic, no one would trust anyone! Everyone would be shifty and guarded and . . . cynical."

"Well, thank god for stupid people, then," Mike said. "*I* don't want everyone to be smart. What a boring world *that* would be. Guys like us wouldn't stand a chance."

"Not guys like us. Guys like you."

"Fine. Guys like me. But do you see my point?"

For a moment, Garth couldn't keep track of the point he was trying to make. His own reasoning seemed to be circling back on itself, redirected by what Mike was saying; it was like a snake eating its own tail. He said, "So you want people to trust you, but that makes them 'stupid,' and you don't respect 'stupid' people. Where does that leave you?"

Mike sat back on the couch. He raised his eyebrows, waiting. "You had a question?"

"Yeah. But before I ask it, I want to tell you, too, that, while I'm grateful for how you nudged me to get to know Adam, I'm also really mad that you took Adam's—*and* his grandfather's—money. They were just saying hi," Garth emphasized. "That's all. You pushed them into buying tickets."

"I didn't push anyone. Do I need to remind you of why we were out there in the first place?"

"*No.* But do you see what I mean? Even if everything else was taken out of the equation, even if we were both the happiest scammers in the world, couldn't you just let them go, make *fifteen dollars* less that day and not embarrass us and ruin my prospects with Adam?"

"I didn't ruin anything," Mike countered. "That

drunken numskull Marcus sent the whole deal top-pling. Plus Jackie and her big mouth. But think about what you're asking me. Are you saying that *maybe* it was okay to take everyone else's money but not theirs? Because that sounds a little skewed."

"I'm not saying *any* of it was okay!" Garth snapped. "I just don't get it. I just don't see— I mean, how much money did we raise, anyway? All three scams, sum to-tal."

"A pretty penny." Mike had one leg crossed over the other. The elevated foot was stirring the air now. His mouth, during the pauses in between his speech, was locked into place by a clenched jaw.

"I'm just thinking it can't have been *that* much money—not life-changing money—when you put it all together, and I don't understand why you'd want to go to all this trouble. I know you want to help us out, but why like this?"

"That's your burning question?" Mike cleared his throat. When he spoke again, his voice was at a vol-ume several notches louder than before. "You know, when I pulled up in front of your place, I knew the three of us weren't so close precisely because *I* wasn't that tight with your dad before he died. And I know I *own* a big part of that. And when I started talking to you and finding out what's really going on, I thought,

Look at him. He's a great guy. And he's afraid to walk around in his own skin because his mom is sending out signals that the world's going to beat him up if he opens his mouth. All due respect to your mom, but at your age you should be learning how to *enjoy* the world. How to grab it with both hands and see how great, how much fun it can really be." He paused and took a deep breath. "So if your burning question is, 'Hey, Mike, why'd you take an interest in my well-being, and why'd you suggest scamming as a way of helping us out?' the answer's pretty cut and dry: because I care about the former, and because I enjoy the latter. It makes me feel alive, okay? *It's what I do.*"

"Actually," Garth said, "the burning question is, 'Where's the money?'"

Mike's entire body—right down to his swirling foot and his expression—froze for a moment. Then the foot resumed its motion. He shifted his head from one side to the other. "Do you honestly think I'd steal from you?"

"I'm just asking."

"After all we've been through together, you think I'd steal—"

"You *taught* me how to steal!" Garth snapped. "Why *wouldn't* I think that? By your own reasoning, I'd be stupid to trust you. Stupid me, right? I overheard those phone calls you made to Stu and whoever it was—Marty—and it sounded like you have a debt to pay off. So I'm just wondering, where's the money we raised?"

"Man," Mike said, and let his gaze drift toward the window. "Man, oh man. You never know where the day's going to take you. Suspected by my own nephew. That stings."

He wasn't answering the question. He was shaking his head, wobbling his foot, shrugging his shoulders in dismay. But he wasn't answering the question.

Garth opened his mouth to ask it again—but before he could, there was a loud pounding on the front door. Hutch scrambled, jumped down to the floor, and began to bark.

"Police!" a voice yelled. "Open up!"

"Oh, no," Mike said. He stared wide-eyed at the door for a moment. He moved toward it, but hesitated. He glanced at the hallway, the kitchen, the back door.

"Police!" the voice hollered again.

"Oh, no," Mike repeated, then dropped his voice to a whisper as he took hold of Garth's arm. "Do me a huge favor. Don't answer that, okay?"

"But—"

"Don't answer it. There's no law that says you have

to answer a door when someone knocks, is there? Not that I know of, anyway. Just don't answer. No one's home! You've got to do this for me."

The pounding continued. Mike pulled Garth into a hug and whispered into his ear, "You're a really good kid. I don't blame you for being suspicious."

A moment later, he'd disappeared down the hall and into his room.

Surely their voices—maybe even their footsteps—had been heard from the front porch. As Hutch continued to bark, Garth felt the panic rising within him. Would they just knock all afternoon if he never answered? Would they break the door down?

He stepped toward it. Took a deep breath. Flinched as the pounding grew louder, and finally reached forward and unlocked the dead bolt.

When he'd opened it only a few inches, he peered out at a narrow blade of a face, a shock of white-blond hair, a spray of whiskers sprouting on the chin.

Jackie's boyfriend.

He wasn't dressed in a police uniform, but he was holding a badge.

He was huffing and hard-eyed, peering into the apartment over the top of Garth's head. Thankfully, he was alone.

"You're not the police," Garth said.

"I'm a security guard," the boyfriend snarled. He stuffed the badge into the back pocket of his jeans. "It opens doors. Where is that slimy, lying bastard?"

"He's not here."

"Like hell he's not. Tell him to step outside. Tell him I want to talk to him."

"Listen . . ." Garth grappled for words. "This is private property. I'll—I'll call the *real* police if you don't leave."

"Come out, you wuss!" the guy shouted over Garth's head.

Could this situation get any worse? Garth wondered.

Of course it could. Things could *always* get worse. Things seemed made, by their very design, to get worse.

A car rolled to a stop in front of the house.

The station wagon. His mom: home from work and already getting out from behind the wheel, her eyes on the porch and her face a billboard for concern, confusion, and worry.

16

"**W**ho are you?" she asked, coming up the steps.

Jackie's boyfriend spun around as if Mike might have suddenly materialized. His hands were still drawn into fists. "The guy who's kicking ass and taking names," he said.

Garth stepped out of the apartment and shut the door behind him.

"What is this about?" his mom asked. "Garth, open the door."

"He wants to see Mike," Garth said, still holding on to the doorknob, "but Mike's not here."

"The hell he's not," the boyfriend said.

"Mike's not here?" his mom asked.

Garth shook his head.

"That's a load of crap. He hit on her *and* he cheated her out of her pay. The whole raffle was one big con job. I'm telling you, I'm not leaving here till I lay into the son of a bitch."

She looked from the boyfriend to Garth and could no doubt tell from the sinking look on her son's face that there was some weight to the accusation. Her shoulders lifted as she drew in a breath. "I don't know what you're talking about or who 'she' is," she said, turning back to the boyfriend, "but if you're taking names, take this one: Sonja Rudd. I live here, and *I'm* telling *you* that if my son says Mike isn't home, he isn't home. You have a foul mouth and you're not intimidating anyone with it. Please leave."

Wow, Garth thought. He'd been expecting inquiry, panic, even outrage. He stepped aside and gazed at her with admiration as she opened the door.

"You," she said out the side of her mouth, "inside."

He was following in her wake when he felt a skinny hand closing around his forearm.

"You were there, too. I saw you in his car when you came and picked her up. I was going to come after you, too, only you're just a shrimp and Jackie told me you'd been twisted, like her. Now that I look at you, I'm not so sure."

"Don't"—Garth jerked his arm free and then shoved both hands against the boyfriend's chest—"call me shrimp."

The guy didn't weigh much. He danced backward down the three steps and barely managed to keep his footing when he got to the sidewalk.

Garth slammed the front door behind him.

When he turned around, his mom was standing in the middle of the living room, staring at him.

"That was quite a performance."

"Yeah, that guy was a psycho."

She dropped her purse and car keys onto the armchair. "I was talking about you. Where is your uncle, anyway?"

"I—I didn't think he should come out. I thought there might be a fight."

"He's letting you fend off his problems now? *Mike!*" she called, glancing into the kitchen and then walking down the hall toward the guest room. "We need to talk."

Garth sank down onto the couch. He stared at Hutch, lying on the floor next to the coffee table, and dreaded the argument that was about to erupt from the back of the apartment. The dog offered him a sticky-eyed look of concern.

Let's see you smooth your way out of this one, Mike.

But when his mom came back into the room, she was alone. "Something you want to tell me?" she asked. "Your uncle really isn't here."

"He's not?"

"His things are gone, too."

"You're kidding."

"Do I look like I'm in the mood to be making jokes? There are a couple of books in there, and his dirty sheets, but that's it."

When did he pack? Garth wondered—and then realized it had to have been while he was over at Lisa's house. Which meant Mike had already decided to leave before Garth had confronted him. He must have crept out the back door while Garth was on the porch.

Garth stood.

"Where are you going?"

"I just want to check something. One sec."

He walked into the kitchen, leaned forward over the sink, and looked through the window at Stafford Avenue. The Camaro was gone.

"I don't understand," he muttered—though, in fact, the situation was becoming all too clear to him. He turned around.

She nodded toward the couch. "Neither do I, but I'm going to. Because you're going to explain it to me, right now. For starters, who in the world is Jackie?"

His mom was a tougher audience than Lisa had been. She wasn't just shocked; she was aghast. She wasn't just dismayed; she was horrified. And she wasn't just irritated by his participation in the scams; she was livid.

"Wait a minute," she said when he was in the middle of telling her about the dog scam, "what day of the week did this happen?"

"A Monday," he said. "The shelter's closed on Mondays, so Ms. Kessler is only there in the mornings and evenings, to feed the dogs and let them out. So she didn't know we borrowed a couple."

"How did you manage that? You work on Mondays."

Which was how she found out he'd quit his job at Peterson's nearly three weeks ago.

Halfway through his recounting their meeting Jackie in The Single Slice, she interrupted him again. "You didn't ever go to any of those historic sites, did you? Those museums and local attractions?"

"No," he admitted.

"I wondered where all the sudden interest in history was coming from. Turns out it wasn't coming from anywhere. How big of a fool does that make me?"

"You're not a fool, Mom."

"Not anymore. I guess I'm going to have to start questioning everything you say."

"You don't have to do that!"

"Never mind. We'll get to that later, after I sort all this— Hold on . . . he took you to a *bar*?"

And so it went. She listened and questioned, listened

and challenged, her brain leapfrogging around as she tried to keep track. And she got angrier by the minute. "So you thought this was a better way to earn money for your college fund than having an actual job?"

"Mike guaranteed the money would beat minimum wage. And it was better than shoveling rats for that creep, Mr. Peterson."

"You told me you liked Mr. Peterson. You told me you liked that job."

"Well, I didn't. I couldn't have hated it—or him—more."

She sat back in the armchair and massaged one of her temples. "And you honestly thought you'd be able to *do* something with this money—pay for tuition and buy books—with a clear conscience? That you'd be able to live with yourself?"

In truth, he hadn't thought that far ahead. Mike, he realized, had had the effect of rendering the present as the only moment in existence, damn the future, damn the past. Now that he was gone, the present felt more damned than anything else. Unable to answer her question, Garth repeated instead, "Mike guaranteed—"

"He *guaranteed*? I wouldn't bet two cents on any guarantee or promise from Mike. Your dad was right about him. This is why I tell you not to trust people with your secrets, with your private business. Because you've got people out there like your uncle who are looking to squeeze whatever they can out of you. I have to say I'm glad Mike's not here right now or I'd put my hands on his throat."

Any other time, the image of his mom trying to strangle someone would have been comically absurd; at the moment, she looked angry enough to do it.

"Look me in the eye and tell me something: Exactly when did you get it into your head that it was okay to lie to every single person in your life?"

"I don't *know!*" he said. "You've just been working so hard lately, and I wanted to do *some*thing to contribute more than just my pathetic salary."

"Don't try to make this about me, Garth. This is about you, and your uncle."

"You know what? It *is* about you, Mom. As much as it's about Mike and me, it's about us."

"And how do you figure that?"

"Because—" He dragged his hands through his hair, then sat forward and anchored his elbows against his knees. "This is the twenty-first century."

"Thanks for the update. What does the century have to do with anything?"

"I'm not going to keep living in the closet! Do you know what the last four months have been like for me? Living a lie about who I am, not even discussing it with you—like it's some kind of secret, when I tried *not* to make it a secret so you and I wouldn't grow apart? And knowing my *mom* was the one who wanted that?"

She looked down at her lap. "You certainly seem to have been capable of living a lie and keeping secrets *lately*."

"That's what I'm saying! Maybe one thing made the other possible."

"I don't think that's fair. I try the best I can with you, and I think you know that."

"And I think *you* know I can't stand hiding who I am! I'm not asking you to march in some 'gay pride' parade with me, or put a rainbow sticker on your car, or tell your boss, 'I have a gay son.' Just try to accept the fact that I can survive being who I am."

"I *have* accepted who you are," she said evenly. Without looking up, she added, "I just haven't dealt with it yet."

He was both nervous and upset. He was forgetting to breathe. He sucked in air, and chose his words carefully. "Lisa knows."

"How does Lisa know?"

"Because I'd already told her before I made my promise to you. And my friend Adam knows, too. He's the one I was with the other night, when I was supposed to be at Lisa's."

"I see."

"I like him," he said. "A lot. Like, I want to date him. But I don't know if he ever wants to see me again."

That last part had slipped out in the heat of the moment. He'd already decided the story was colorful enough without mentioning that Adam and his grand-dad had been at the fairgrounds to witness the raffle disaster.

Thankfully, his mom didn't ask what he'd meant by the remark.

"How did you meet him?"

"Through Mike."

"What did *Mike* have to do with it?"

In for a penny, in for a pound. "He took me to the gay bookstore near Carytown. He bought me some novels and magazines and a really cool movie—don't worry, none of it was dirty. He saw how miserable I was, and he did something about it."

"So he did all that, knowing how I felt," she observed.

"He thought Dad would have wanted—"

"Mike doesn't know a damn thing about what your dad would have wanted. They weren't close enough for him to have known. And that's beside the point, anyway. It's not Mike's place to take things into his own hands like that."

"But do you see what I'm saying, Mom? I know I promised not to tell anyone, but it was killing me. And Mike saw that. I couldn't make any gay friends, I couldn't . . ."

"As I've tried to make clear," she said, "you aren't big enough to defend yourself if someone—"

"What if this is as tall as I ever get?" he snapped. He'd obsessed over that worry a million times, but he'd never spoken it aloud. "It could happen, you know. Should I stay a closeted little freak for the rest of my life? Do you want me to be miserable?"

"Of course not." Her eyes were damp now, he noticed. So were his. She got up from the armchair and moved to the couch beside him. When she reached out and put her hand on his shoulder, he flinched. "Since when did you become so jumpy around me?"

"I just don't feel like being touched right now, is all."

"Listen to me. I hate seeing you like this. So we'll deal with it. Okay? We'll talk about it. The gay thing, I mean. As for the other . . ." She hesitated, and looked away.

He thought maybe she was crying; but when her head swung back around, her jaw was set forward and her eyes had hardened and she looked angrier than ever. "I'm surprised the two of you didn't end up in jail. I'll tell you one trait your dad and your uncle Mike shared: pride. Mike is too proud to ever stoop to working at a regular job, with a boss, so he drifts around gambling and meddling with who knows how many people's lives. As for your dad . . ." She held him in her gaze, but her words trailed off.

"What about Dad?"

"Your dad was too proud to admit he could do any wrong."

"Meaning . . ."

"That second hardware store was a mistake. Everyone makes mistakes, that's normal. But he was already in over his head, and when he realized it, he only made things worse thinking another store would help. He didn't even tell *me* how bad things were, because he was too proud to admit he'd taken a wrong turn. We wouldn't have been in nearly as bad a shape if he'd just stayed with the place on Hamilton. But he refused. He spent and he borrowed and he spent some more. And then . . . he died."

It was shocking to hear her state it so bluntly.

"I'm angry at your dad," she said.

"But he's—"

"I know. He's not here to be angry at. That's one of the things that makes me angry. I miss him, of course, and I want him back every day of my life. But he left us in a big mess."

She took a deep breath and folded her arms across her stomach. "So where is all this stolen money that was supposedly for your college fund, anyway?"

Garth cringed. He stared at Hutch, who had the luxury of simply falling asleep. "Mike has it."

"Mike has the money," his mom said.

He nodded. "He kept saying he was keeping it all together, and that we were going to tell you we bought a lucky lottery ticket and surprise you with one lump sum."

"Brilliant. Did it occur to you, like it would have to me, that unless you win a dollar or two from a scratch-off card, the state doesn't pay you in *cash*? They issue a check. A government check. How much money are we talking about, anyway?"

"I don't know. I never actually saw it all put together."

She shook her head and stood up from her chair. "I can only hope he uses it to travel as far away from Richmond as he can."

"What are you doing?"

"Making a cup of tea," she said. "It's all I want in the world, right now. A quiet cup of tea."

"Well, what about me?"

"I'm mad at you. You can get your own tea."

"No, I mean . . . am I grounded, or what?"

"Let's see." She counted off his offenses on the fingers of one hand. "You lied about where you were the other night. You broke your promise about not coming out yet. Oh, yes—you participated in an ongoing fraud and cheated who knows how many innocent people out of their money. I'd say you're grounded until you turn . . . forty. Not that we're done talking about it." Her eyes fell to the end table. "Why am I looking at a Christmas present?"

"It's a ship model Mike gave me. He said it was the only wrapping paper he could find."

"A model," she said. "Which is supposed to be what, a consolation prize?"

"It's the *Flying Dutchman*."

"Perfect," she said. "At least he has a sense of humor." She walked into the kitchen.

He wandered into the backyard, his hands jammed into his pockets, feeling miserable about their conversation (which, as she'd pointed out, was unfinished), miserable about himself, about Adam, and perhaps most of all miserable about Mike.

Mike, who had skipped out while Garth was confronting Jackie's angry boyfriend, which meant he hadn't really cared whether or not the guy took a swing at his fifteen-year-old nephew.

Mike, who had either had a last-minute, greedy change of heart or who had been planning all along to steal the money.

Mike, who had orchestrated an entire network of lies and had somehow convinced Garth to go along.

Hutch had followed him outside. The spaniel visited a few choice spots along the hedges, then found his filthy tennis ball and carried it back to Garth, where he dropped it and looked up expectantly.

Where was it Mike had said he was headed the night he'd first arrived?

Atlantic City.

They could follow him there. Get into the station wagon and drive, their eyes peeled for that sleek blue Camaro with the grinning con man behind the wheel and the overnight bag filled with cash in the trunk.

And what if they caught up with him? Hold him against a chain-link fence, maybe. Slip the end of a knife blade inside one of his nostrils. *Do you like your nose, Mike? Do you like breathing through it?*

But no. There wasn't much of a violent streak in Garth. He couldn't even enjoy fantasizing about it.

Hutch barked in frustration, nudged the ball, stepped back from it.

Garth brought his foot back and kicked it across the yard.

Back inside, he carried Mike's gift to his room, sat on his bed, and tore the snowman paper away from the box. He didn't understand his mom's remark about how Mike still had his sense of humor intact until he removed the lid, opened the booklet that came with the model, and compared what it said there to what Mike had told him weeks ago about the legend of the *Flying Dutchman*.

In Mike's version, the crew of the *Dutchman* was cursed to sail the seas giving aid to ships in peril—forever and ever, till the end of time. According to the booklet that came with the model, the *Dutchman* had been caught in a storm off the Cape of Good Hope, and when a divine angel had appeared on the bow to offer help, the captain had taken a shot at it. From that point on, the *Dutchman* was doomed to wander without rest, and to bring down disaster on any ship within its path.

17

For the first time since Mike's arrival, Garth dreamed of his dad on the Chesapeake Bay, and for the first time since the accident, the dreamed changed. Mr. Holt wasn't even in it. Garth was the one manning the tiller. His dad was working the line for the sail. They were enjoying themselves, tacking across the surface, watching gulls circle and dive, circle and dive, some of them bobbing up out of the water with fish twisting in their beaks.

Right on cue, the storm came out of nowhere. It darkened the sky and brought with it a harsh, battering wind. The rain soaked them to the skin within minutes. Then things—as Garth knew they would—turned serious, fast. *Dad,* he shouted over the noise, *this is bad. I know what happens. We're going to drown.*

No, we're not, his dad hollered back. *Head east!*

Garth pulled on the tiller, and the boat turned.

The wind caught the sail. They were practically flying across the water. It sluiced away on either side, and even the storm seemed to have a hard time keeping up with them. Garth steered with one hand, held on to the Sunfish's side with the other, and yelled, *Why am I not seasick? Is it because this isn't really happening?*

It's happening, his dad yelled back. *It's real. Look up ahead!*

Garth leaned sideways, peering around the mast and the sail, through the rain, to a blinking yellow eye fixed over a dark spot on the horizon. The spot grew, and gradually it took the shape of a dock.

The mainland. They were going to make it, he realized.

They were going to live.

He'd spent several hours steeped in thought the night before, unable to fall asleep. As a result, when he opened his eyes from the dream, it was midmorning, nearly ten o'clock.

His mom had left for work over an hour ago. The note taped to the milk jug read

> *Don't forget you're grounded and in very big trouble. No television. No fun of any kind. No stepping outside the apartment—unless the place is on fire or you want to take Hutch for a walk.*
> *Love, Mom.*

There was at least a hint of humor there. He scrambled an egg and ate it between two slices of toast with ketchup. Because he'd been forbidden to turn on the television, he sat with the newspaper at the kitchen table and read the comics. Then he washed his dishes and returned to his room, still haunted by the dream. What did it mean? Had it been his tiller work or his dad's handling of the sail that had saved them? Did it matter? He hadn't been drenched in sweat when he'd awakened; his heart hadn't been pounding. One of those corny interpretation books might have told him the dream meant *survival.* Another one might say, *Water represents change, but rain represents sadness.* Garth had never believed that stuff and didn't believe it now. How about this: *Dreaming that you and your dad were in a boat and didn't drown means: Lucky you for having the dream.*

Still, it seemed like there had to be some connection between recent events and what his sleeping mind had conjured up.

Eager to make whatever amends were possible with his mom, he got out the cleaning supplies and scrubbed down the hall bathroom. He vacuumed and dusted the living room. He made his bed and straightened up his closet, said, "To hell with eBay," to Hutch, and carried all the Halloween costumes out to one of the garbage bins alongside the building (save for the capeless

Superman outfit, which, as far as he knew, was still on the floor of the rental car). Finally, he stuck his head into the room opposite his—what had so suddenly become "Mike's room" and then, just as suddenly, gone back to being "the spare room."

On the ladder-back chair sat the dog-eared copies of *Double Indemnity* and *The Big Sleep*. He picked them both up and read the back covers, but decided he'd had enough of crime for a while and so set them back down.

The sheets Mike had used were in a wad on the floor at the foot of the daybed. Garth gathered them up and dropped them into the washer, then wandered back to his room. The HMS *Victory* sat on his desk, officially completed, its sails glued into place. He'd taken his time with the model, and he had to admit it looked pretty great. Carefully, he edged the *Batavia* to one side on top of his dresser, turned it at a diagonal to make room, then lifted the *Victory* from his desk and carried it over. With the two ships arranged so that their bowsprits pointed at each other, they looked to be on a collision course, so he lined them up parallel, bowsprits aimed toward the window. That way, they appeared to be racing—or just sailing side by side.

He turned around, and was caught somewhat off guard by the sight of his barren desk: no project in the works, just the X-ACTO knife, the sandpaper, and the few other tools and model supplies that remained there all summer when there was no schoolwork to do. Should he start on the *Flying Dutchman*? Should he work on it at all? The model itself looked highly detailed and fairly complex. But was it better just to toss out a "consolation prize" from Mike after all that had happened rather than have the finished product—impressive as it would undoubtedly be—staring him in the face, reminding him of how he'd stood around in public dressed as Superman and Scooby-Doo while he lied and helped steal from both strangers and friends?

He told himself he was indifferent to the decision.

And, besides, maybe it was time to give up the ship models entirely. When he'd glimpsed them in the mirror the night he and Adam had watched *Beautiful Thing,* they'd looked like nothing more than a bunch of childish toys.

He carried the box, which rattled with the unassembled parts of the *Flying Dutchman,* down the hall and through the living room, bound for the back door. The dryer buzzed as he was passing.

He set the box on the kitchen counter and pulled the dryer door open. He was removing the sheets when a T-shirt crackled with static electricity and dropped to the floor. Bright yellow. A green, grinning dragon on the front, eating ice cream.

Mike. For all of Mike's many, many faults, Garth wanted the T-shirt. Even if he could never wear it around his mom.

He also wanted the model of the *Flying Dutchman*.

He let Hutch out into the backyard, then carried the box and the T-shirt back to his room. He folded the shirt and tucked it into the bottom drawer of his dresser. He set the box down in front of him on his bed. The booklet still lay on top of the pieces, opened to where he'd been reading the legend.

So I'll build it, he thought. *If nothing else, it'll be a monument to a low point in my life.*

He began removing the plastic racks of pieces from the box and laying them out on his desk.

Hutch barked at the back door, ready to be let back in.

"I'm coming!" he hollered.

The dog barked again.

"I said I'm coming! Don't lose your fur—"

He stopped, midsentence. When the dog barked a third time, he hardly heard him.

Lisa slapped the side of his computer monitor. "Does this thing even work?"

"*Yes.* You just have to give it about a year to boot up. Why? What's so important to show me? Pictures of your latest boyfriend?"

"Very funny," she said. "I want to show you something I made for *you.*"

"Wow—what is it?"

"You'll see. Meanwhile, why did you ask me over? You sounded all frantic when you called."

"Two reasons," Garth told her. "One, I'm not allowed to leave the house because I'm grounded due to my recent criminal high jinks."

"Yes, yes, I'll slip you a file inside a Twinkie. Why else?"

"Because of this."

The money—which Mike had changed out into mostly twenty-dollar bills—was rubber-banded together and resting beneath one-half of the *Flying Dutchman*'s hull. There was a post-it note attached that read simply:

> *You deserve to be the one who presents this to her.–Mike*

Garth lifted the inch-high stack and waved it at Lisa.

"Oh my god!" she said, her eyes widening. "This is what you made?"

"Yeah. It's crazy, right?"

"It's beyond crazy. How much is it?"

"Two thousand eight hundred and seventeen bucks."

"Amazing," she said. "See, that's the ultracrazy part—that there are that many people who would believe a pair of dorks standing next to a card table."

"I'm not a dork! And, besides, it's not like twenty-eight hundred people each gave us a dollar; some of them gave us five or ten. One old guy shelled out fifty!"

She shook her head. "So the Flying Jerkman didn't make off with the loot after all?"

"Not much of it, anyway. He may have skimmed some for travel expenses."

"He was probably planning to vanish with every penny, then chickened out when you confronted him."

Not so, Garth knew. He'd replayed the sequence of events in his mind over and over again: He'd made it clear to Mike that he was done scamming; Mike had conceded; then he'd presented Garth with the *Flying Dutchman,* already wrapped, the cash hidden inside. All of that *before* Garth had challenged him about the money's whereabouts. Even if he'd secretly packed his things and had been planning on making a stealthy exit, taking the money with him hadn't been part of his plan.

She glanced at his computer again. "Finally!" she said, and then opened a connection to the internet. "Check your email."

"I never get email."

"Because you never *write* email. But check. I sent you something."

He logged on to his account and saw over thirty new messages, nearly every one of them junk. But the most recent one was from Lisa. "Sometimes You Feel Like a Nut," read the subject line. He opened it, clicked on the attachment, and then listened to the cricket sounds of his computer struggling with the file. As slowly as if a tapestry were being woven down the screen from top to bottom, the picture opened.

There was his dad, hunched down next to the base of the tree, holding a peanut for the blurry squirrel. Only, the squirrel wasn't quite as blurry as it had been in the snapshot. And the evidence of the creases was gone, the flecks of color that had fallen away over the years filled in with some expert Photoshopping. Jerry Rudd, at about the same age Garth was now, looked vibrant and glowing. The picture might have been taken yesterday.

"How did you get this?"

"You handed me the snapshot the other day, remember? I didn't give it back. I wanted to hold on to it and make a reproduction for you. If you had a printer—or if I had one that didn't keep breaking down—we could print it out on glossy paper, eight by ten, and get it framed."

"This looks great!"

"I know," she said proudly.

"Hey, thanks, Lisa. A *lot*."

"You're welcome a lot. Here's the original, by the way." She took a small envelope out of her purse and handed it to him.

"I can't wait to show my mom. She's going to love it. I might make it my screen saver, too."

"So . . ." Lisa's eyes had moved from the computer screen back to the bed, and the stack of money. "What happens to all of *that*?"

"We could go to Kings Dominion for a month."

"*No.*"

"You're right, it would probably get boring after day seven. How about we buy two new printers—one for me and one for you?"

"Garth, you can't spend this money! You can't keep it! It's stolen."

"I know, I know. But what am I going to do? It's not like I can give it back to all those people. I don't even know who they were."

"You have to give it to your mom," Lisa told him.

"She won't take it! She'll be horrified."

"No, I mean, give it to your mom and let *her* decide. What other choice do you have?"

He stared at the money. He nodded. "You're right. Still"—he reached down and ran his thumb along the edge of the stack—"just a hundred? Who would know? We could go to a movie, buy the newest Sufjan, maybe order a pizza with about twenty toppings?"

"I hope you're kidding. The last thing you need to do right now is juggle any more karma knives. Have you talked to Adam, by the way?"

"*No.* I wasn't planning to. I think I'm more or less an ass in his eyes now."

"Not an ass. A thief. I talked to him."

"You called him? And he said I was a *thief*? This is worse than standing around in those stupid costumes, worse than the guilt, worse even than having my mom so mad at me—"

"Would you calm down, Spasmatic? In the first place, he called me. In the second place, *thief* was my word, not his."

"Thanks."

"Let me clarify: he doesn't think you're an ass, or a horrible person. He thinks you *stole*. Which you did. But I worked my magic and did my best to convince him that that wasn't the regular you. I tried to convince him that Uncle Cesspool practically forced you to do it."

"That's not really true."

"I know. Adam didn't believe it, either. But I made a good case. And he knows it's not his place to bring down the gavel. He just isn't sure he wants to get more . . . involved with you."

"He said that?"

"In so many words."

"What did you tell him?"

"I gave you a C minus for caving under the influence of a bad uncle, and an A plus for being a friend who is *mortified* that he could have done such a thing, and who wants to make it up to everyone. How's that?"

"Thanks. I guess."

"You should call him."

"I can't do that. I'd be wondering what expression he had on his face while I fumbled for what to say. It would be horrible."

"So go over to his house. Talk to him live and in person."

"No way."

"Think about it, at least. You've got nothing to lose, right? I mean, the karma knives are already spinning circles over your head as it is."

"You have a really funny way of consoling people. Speaking of karma knives: What's the latest with your brother and Stacy? Are your parents still pushing for the you know what?"

"No. That's totally off the discussion table. I mean, Stacy never would have done it, anyway, but then she got her sonogram, and that itty-bitty picture changed everything. The whole pack of them is gung ho now, full speed ahead."

"Because it was so cute?"

She shook her head. "Twins. Like *that* makes any difference."

He made tuna casserole that night (the ingredients, surprisingly enough, were already in the cabinets, and the recipe looked easy to follow). He served the meal, cleared the plates, and washed the dishes. His mom stayed at the table and watched him work. He was putting plastic wrap around the leftovers when she said, "I appreciate the meal. And all the housecleaning."

He nodded as he held the casserole dish with both hands and opened the refrigerator with his foot.

"But you're still in big trouble."

"I know," he said.

"And we still have a lot to talk about."

"I know," he said again, "but can you give me just a second? I'll be right back."

"Sure."

He closed the fridge and walked to his room.

When he came back into the kitchen, he set the stack of money on the table in front of her.

She sprang out of her chair as if he'd presented her with a scorpion. "Oh my god," she said, staring at the bills. "Where did this . . . did Mike come back here?"

"No, I think he's gone for good, Mom. But he didn't take that, like I thought he did. He left it in the ship model he gave me."

She sat back down, one hand covering her mouth. With her other hand, she flipped through the bills. "It's stolen property. I mean, it may as well be stolen. I *still* cannot believe you took part in this."

"Don't I even get any points for not just keeping my mouth shut when I discovered it?"

"*No.*" She shook her head, staring at the money. "People don't get rewarded for not doing the wrong thing. People get rewarded for doing the right thing. Although I'm glad you didn't keep your mouth shut. It gives me hope that you might still have a head on your shoulders."

Might.

"Lord," she said. Her shoulders sank back against the chair. "I don't know what to do."

"We could add it to my college fund. I won't touch it, I promise."

"We can't put this money into your college fund! We can't keep it, Garth. Can't you see that? It doesn't belong to us."

"Well, we can't return it to the people it came from, either."

"No, you and your uncle made that pretty much impossible, didn't you?"

He sat down across from her. After a moment, he said, "We could give it to the police."

"I was just thinking that. But it's not an option."

"Why?"

"Because what you and Mike did was highly illegal, and the police would want an explanation for where this all came from. If I tell them about Mike, or any of the places where you two pulled your stunts, they could go around asking questions and that could put them on a trail that leads right back to you. We're talking about, what, hundreds of eyewitnesses?"

"I was in costumes for some of it," he said. "People probably didn't get such a good look at me."

"I wish you were in one now," she snapped. "I wish you were in the Garth costume you used to wear before that con man came to town. I *miss* the Garth costume, I really do."

"You know what?" he said, suddenly angry. "That's just what it was, Mom: a costume. Because every day I

314 •

was pretending to be somebody the world would have an easier time *accepting*."

"That was for your own good."

"It was for *your* own good! So *you* could worry less! It made me miserable, and you didn't care—"

Her eyes had gone slightly damp yet again. He didn't want to make her cry: he didn't need one more thing to feel guilty about.

"Never mind," he said, pushing up from the table. "Give the money away. Burn it. I don't care. But just so you know, I'm done with the costumes—*all* of them, including the one you want me to wear."

He left the kitchen, stormed off down the hall, and slammed his bedroom door, expecting her to follow.

To his surprise, she didn't.

The next day, he retreated to his room as soon as she got home from work and stayed there with his door closed. After a while, he heard voices—the television, he thought. Good for her; she could watch TV because she wasn't grounded for the next twenty-five years. Then he realized there was only voice, and it was hers. She was on the telephone. Calling Grandma Rudd, maybe, to complain about what had happened with Mike. He eased his door open to eavesdrop, but she'd fallen nearly silent by then and was only humming yes and no; whoever was on the other end of the line was doing most of the talking.

Just before sundown, she knocked on his door.

"It's open," he said. He was sitting at his desk, assembling the hull of the *Flying Dutchman*.

She stuck her head in. "Leftovers for dinner, all right?"

"Stomachache."

"Did anyone ever tell you you're a bad liar?"

"No. They tell me I'm quite good at it, in fact. It must be because I've had so much practice." He didn't look at her as he said this. He stared at the hunk of plastic in his hands.

She said, "I *am* making an effort here, you know."

"Are you?"

"Yes. You just don't know it yet. So don't be too mean, or you're going to feel really terrible about it later, okay?"

He looked over. She was staring at him intently, waiting for him to respond.

"Okay," he said.

She closed the door.

The next morning, there wasn't a note taped to the milk jug. There was a letter—in a proper envelope, bearing his first name in her handwriting—propped between the salt and pepper shakers on the kitchen table.

He let Hutch out, poured himself a large bowl of cereal, and sat down. For the length of time it took him to eat, he just stared at the envelope without opening it. *What was the worst thing it could say?* That she could never forgive him for what he'd done? That she was turning him in to the police in order to teach him a lesson? That she was certifiably insane with worry? *Just open the damn letter.*

He did.

> *Dear Garth,*
>
> *First off, I hate being mad at you. Second, Mike was very, very wrong when he came up with the idea for what you two did. And while I firmly believe in forgiveness, it's going to take me a long time to be able to forgive him. But I want you to forgive him, and I want you to learn from what happened.*
>
> *Please know: I'll always worry about you getting hurt. To my mind, I'd be a bad mom if I didn't. But I don't want this "wall" you mentioned to stand between us any longer. Hard as it is for me to admit, Mike was right about how you should be able to be true to yourself, and to other people. And I can't stand the thought of*

being excluded from a major part of your life.
I've been thinking about our first conversation
about your being gay, and I've been remember-
ing what I was like at your age. No one could
have told me—much less convinced me—to
behave differently from how I felt. And it isn't
realistic for me to ask that of you now.

He reread this last sentence twice and thought, *Amazing.* She finally saw where he was coming from; she'd just had to reach that point on her own.

I want you to be who you are around me,
and around other people you trust. That doesn't
mean everyone under the sun, but your friends
and anyone you might be interested in dating.
I also want you to have the support network a
person your age needs. By that I mean not just
people who will listen to you, but people who
can offer guidance and real information.

Last night, I called ROSMY. I've made an
appointment for the two of us to meet with a
counselor this evening, if you want to go. So I'm
trying, Garth. And I need you to be patient with
me, okay? Let's take it one step at a time. The
appointment is for 7:30 p.m. I know you don't

have any other plans, since you aren't forty yet and are still grounded (ha-ha). We can eat a quick dinner together and then go.

Oh—and I've decided what to do with the you-know-what. Since it was given in good faith for charity, I'm giving it away. So if these people tonight seem to be worth their weight in salt, they'll be getting an anonymous donation in the near future.

Don't forget: No television. No fun. And no leaving the apartment unless it's to walk the dog.

Love you with all my heart,

Mom

He read it three times. He refolded it and put it back in the envelope. Then he took it out and read it again. She was trying. She needed him to be patient. Something Adam had said came drifting back into his head.

There really aren't any one-way streets.

He let Hutch back in and went to his room, and for a while he just sat in front the *Flying Dutchman* and stared at the complex network of unassembled pieces. Where was Mike right now? How would he react if he learned that Garth's mom was finally starting to come to terms with who Garth was? How would he react to what she intended to do with all the money they'd raised? And would Lisa be surprised? He thought about picking up the phone and calling her, updating her, asking her advice on how to handle his end of the counseling session . . .

And then, suddenly, calling her was the last thing he wanted to do. No: it was in competition for last place, along with speculating on Mike, on his mom, on what might or might not transpire that evening. His mind had been so crowded lately, but it was tilting now like a listing ship, every thought and image sliding into the water save for one that clutched onto the deck as the ship righted itself.

And what was that one thought? That one image?

Garth Rudd, alone, gripping the tiller and working the line for the sail. Steering into waters that were calm, or not calm.

He walked across the hall to the bathroom, where he turned on the shower. When the water was warm enough, he stood beneath its spray with his eyes closed and tried to hold on to that solitary image.

Naked, he stood against the doorjamb of his room and placed his finger level with the top of his head, then checked it against the mark. It was slightly higher than the mark he'd made just days ago. Was that possible? He got a pen from his desk drawer. Stood against the doorjamb again. Tried not to extend his spine, but tried not to slouch, either. As conservatively as possible, he made a new mark on the painted wood, then turned and examined it. An eighth, maybe even just a sixteenth of an inch higher than the previous mark. But it was something.

He'd take what he could get.

We take what comes, his mom would say, *and we make the most of what we have.*

He dug out the yellow T-shirt with the grinning dragon, and pulled it on. Bicycling to Adam's house would be a blatant violation of his punishment. He stepped into the kitchen, took Hutch's leash from the nail beside the back door, and turned around to find the dog already at his feet, gazing up at him with expectant, sticky eyes.

"Come on," he said. "We're walking."